Fanny Margaret Taylor

A Pearl In Dark Waters

A Tale Of The Times Of Blessed Margaret Mary

Fanny Margaret Taylor

A Pearl In Dark Waters
A Tale Of The Times Of Blessed Margaret Mary

ISBN/EAN: 9783337342739

Printed in Europe, USA, Canada, Australia, Japan

Cover: Foto ©Andreas Hilbeck / pixelio.de

More available books at **www.hansebooks.com**

PEARL IN DARK WATERS.

A Tale of the Times of Blessed Margaret Mary.

BY THE

AUTHOR OF "TYBORNE," "DAME DOLORES," ETC.

NEW YORK:
P. J. KENEDY,
PUBLISHER TO THE HOLY APOSTOLIC SEE,
EXCELSIOR CATHOLIC PUBLISHING HOUSE,
3 AND 5 BARCLAY STREET,
1897.

A PEARL IN DARK WATERS.

CHAPTER I.

ROB'S LAST RIDE.

RITA, Rita, where are you?" exclaimed a ringing, joyous voice; and Robert Viscount Milroy dashed out on the terrace, and then into the garden, in search of his sister. "There you are, stuck away in that summer-house, poring over some stupid book, as usual. I have finished my task. How I hate it, and that tiresome Master Crabhouse. And now I want to have a gallop on Tony, while you ride Bess."

"Oh, Rob, you must not ride Tony," said his sister; "you know my father has said so."

"No such thing," answered the boy, while a hot flush mantled to his brow. "It was nothing but that insolent varlet Isaac's prating to my lord. As if there were any horse in the stables *I* cannot ride. Where is May? I did not think you would be so contrary, Rita," added he, reproachfully.

"I heard my lord's voice," observed Marguerite; and a sudden change came over Robert's face and manner. He hastily took a knife from his pocket, and began to peel the bark from a slip of wood he had picked up from the ground. Marguerite opened her book, and both were quiet and demure-looking enough when their father's stately form appeared at the entrance of the summer-house. Marguerite rose and courtesied; Robert made a respectful bow.

The Earl of Edenhall was a grave, stern-looking man. His features were fine, but there was a restless expression in his eyes, and a twitching about the mouth, which disfigured his face. "Ha, Robert," said he, glancing keenly at his son, "was Master Crabhouse contented with you to-day? Indeed, sir, unless you mend your ways, you will cut a sorry figure in the world, and be fit for nothing but a dunce's cap."

Robert hung his head, and muttered a reply which was quite inaudible. His father apparently cared not to hear it, but, laying his hand on his daughter's head, said, in a softer tone, "Where is May? I thought the twins were like turtle-doves, never apart."

Marguerite, with a smile and blush, answered that her sister was with Mrs. Dorothy, learning to make medicaments. Lord Edenhall's face clouded. "May is too fond of that sort of thing," he said; "on such a spring morning as this she should not be pottering over herbs and stewpans. Go, fetch her, child;" and, in an instant, Marguerite was gone. The Earl strolled on, and, as soon as he disappeared, Robert slipped out of the garden.

The Earl of Edenhall belonged to a family that had remained faithful to the Church and the cause of the Stuarts. His father and two elder brothers fell at Marston Moor, while he was but a stripling, and, as soon as the royal cause was totally lost, the young earl and his mother fled to France. Hardly had Lord Edenhall attained his majority before his mother died, and he was alone

in the world. Upon his lonely, dreary life
the fair Marguerite d'Estries shone like a star.
He married her; and, as his estates were in
possession of the Commonwealth, and her portion was a small one, they were very poor,
but also very happy. Lord Edenhall was
one of those reserved and haughty natures
who love but few, but whose love is so
intense and absorbing that it is not readily
understood by those whose affections are
more diffuse and not so passionate. He held
his wife to be a creature altogether above
ordinary mortals. In truth she was highly
gifted in body and mind, one of those beings
who charm and delight us for awhile, and
then pass from our sight before advancing
life and its cares have robbed them of their
early bloom. It was on a bright 20th of
July that the twin daughters were born,
apparently to make the wedded life of Lord
and Lady Edenhall perfect. There was a
loving discussion how to name them. Margaret had been the name of Lord Edenhall's
mother, it was also that of his wife, while the
babies were born on St. Margaret's Day. It
was a question which of the twins should

bear the name. At last it was settled to give it to both, making Marguerite the name of .he elder, and Margery that of the younger, to distinguish them, if need be, in after years. For daily use the proud young mother called them Rita and May, when she began to prepare for a successor to their cradle.

But the day that saw the birth of Robert was the last of his mother's life; and it was many months before Lord Edenhall could bear to look on the unoffending child whose birth had put an end to his brief happiness.

He fell into gloomy moroseness, and his friends rejoiced when the restoration of Charles II brought him back to his country and his estates, and obliged him once more to mix among men. But sorrow, when it does not enoble a character, generally debases it; and such was the case with Lord Edenhall. Instead of bending under the hand of God in his grief, he had rebelled against it, and his sore and chafing spirit was not prepared to take up the heavy cross that awaited all who in England would be faithful to the Church.

The restoration of Charles had, of course,

roused the hopes of English Catholics that for them good times were at hand. In truth, during the first eighteen years of Charles II's reign there was some cessation from persecution; but poverty, retirement and extreme caution were still their lot. They could take no share in affairs of State; the honors and distinctions of the world were not within their grasp.

Lord Edenhall was keen-sighted, and of rare ability. He saw all this most plainly, and turned his back deliberately on the Faith of his youth. He had his reward. His talents were appreciated; he was called on to take his part in the busy turmoil of court life and politics. The memory of his wife could not check him; it was agony to him to recall the face and voice now lost to him forever on earth. He buried her out of his mental sight, and heaped the earth of incessant occupation and of absorbing thoughts upon her grave.

He left his children in France for many years, not caring to be reminded by their faces and childish talk of the memory of the past. But years crept on. Time did its work—the heart grew harder, and ambition was stronger than sentiment. His heir must not grow up a Frenchman; his daughters, by their marriages, must increase the power and influence of their family. And so, some six months before our story opens, the two Marguerites and their brother were brought to England, and took up their abode at Eden-hall, a large rambling old house, standing in the midst of beautiful Kentish scenery, and not more than forty miles from London. Soon after their arrival, the Earl told his children that no Catholic priests were allowed to minister in England, and that they must carefully avoid the subject of religion in conversation; moreover, he insisted on their appearing with him, from time to time, in the large square pew that had been erected during the Commonwealth in the old church of Edenhall (whitewash having long since hidden the sculpture and decorations of that once fair building). Robert, a thorough boy, intoxicated with the delight of finding himself the possessor of ponies and dogs, and careless and heedless beyond what his tender years might excuse, did not trouble his head about the matter, while the girls were far too much afraid of their father to make any objection; and, as he sat in moody silence in one corner of the pew, while they told their beads in another, they concluded it was as distasteful to him as to them.

The infliction did not take place often. The smallest sign of bad weather, the slightest indisposition of anyone of the party was enough to cause church-going to be given up. Their occasional appearance prevented all suspicion of Papistry attaching to the household, and with that the Earl was satisfied.

In a few minutes Rita returned to the summer-house with her sister. As they could see no traces of either father or brother, they sat down side by side. The sisters were not so much alike as twins often are. Rita was the taller of the two, and her dark eyes were full of brilliant sparkling light, while those of May were soft and dove-like. But both had the same brown hair, with a golden thread running through it, the same delicately-cut features, the same slender and graceful form. Anyone who watched them narrowly would soon perceive that Rita would lead and May would follow —Rita rule and May obey.

"I cannot think why my father should dislike my spending time with Mistress Dorothy," said May. "Surely we ought to know somewhat of medicaments. Lady Rose Hilton makes up salves and potions for all the poor on her land, and for miles around."

"I suppose it is only a whim," returned her sister; "but pray do not displease him, May, for I hope he will take us to London soon. I am wearied to death with this dull place."

"Are you so dull, poor Rita?" said May, stroking her sister's hair under her cap. "I am so sorry! As for me, I am too busy with my flowers, and the chickens I am trying to rear—learning all I can of housewifery from Mistress Dorothy, and my Latin from Master Crabhouse, to have time to be dull; but I *do* want to go to London very much!"

"You are a happy child, May, to amuse yourself with these things. Who would believe I am but a few minutes older than you? But I should like to know why you want to go to London; 'tis only the other day you said the very contrary."

"I did so, Rita, dearest; but Mistress Dorothy hath told me"—here May dropped her voice and looked cautiously round—"Mistress Dorothy says it will be easy to get the Sacraments in London, and here it would be very hard. Sometimes she hath been more than a year without seeing a priest, and then has had to frame some excuse for her absence, and take a long journey. There is a hut, she says, far away in the Clyme Woods, where a priest said Mass once—there were thirty people there—but she says it would be very difficult for you and me to go there."

"I should think so," returned Rita. "But, *petite*, your news about London is no news to me. Do you not know the Queen is a Catholic, and the fair Duchess of York also? And if we are about the Court, nothing can be more easy than to attend the Royal Chapel."

"I wonder," answered May, with a thoughtful look in her gentle eyes, "why the Queen allows us to be so persecuted, since it is her own religion? Why does she not speak to the King? Do not you remember, Rita, how old Louise used to tell us our father would do everything our mother wished? Ah, dear!"—and tears came into May's eyes—"how I wish we had known our mother!"

Rita kissed away the tears. Often, indeed, in their young lives, had the children longed for a mother's smile, a mother's protecting sympathy.

"Well," continued May, "I want to know, Rita—you talk to all the people who come, to whom I never dare speak—but you must know why does not the Queen speak to the King?"

Rita looked gravely at her sister before she answered. "Child, how can I tell? When we go to Court, you will know the reason soon enough. Hush! who is this coming?" as rapid steps were heard approaching. "Oh, Robert, you at last! Where have you been, you look in such a heat?"

"It's too bad!" exclaimed the boy, as he

flung himself into a seat; "am I always to be treated like a child?"

"I suppose it is about this wretched Tony," said Rita, in a despairing tone.

"I had him saddled," cried the boy, eagerly, "and was just about to set off, when who should come slinking in but that spy Isaac. And then it was, *"Oh, my lord, indeed you must not; the Earl hath forbidden;"* and all that stuff. He is a knave, that Isaac, I tell you, Sisters; and, if I had a gold angel to spare, I'll warrant me he would change his tone. As luck will have it, I have spent all my money, and I suppose you two have none to spare," he added, ruefully."

"Certainly not to enable you to break your neck," answered Rita.

"Such nonsense!" returned the boy. "Of course I put up with it from you, because you aré only a girl, and are afraid of my hurting my little finger; but Isaac knows better."

"But if he knows our father hath forbidden it?" said May, in a slow, hesitating voice, as if she had been trying to condemn him for thwarting her darling brother, but was unable to pass sentence. She had no answer. Robert had started up in a listening attitude; his face brightened.

"There, 'tis he!" he cried; "that's Jack's whistle, as a sign that Isaac has gone right down into the village. I'm off."

"O Rob, Rob!" said his sisters, catching hold of him in dismay, "don't do it; it's better not. You might be hurt." But he shook off their grasp, and, with a merry smile and nod, dashed out of sight.

"Oh, I hope he'll come to no harm!" sighed May. "Well," said Rita, recovering herself, "boys will run into danger. I suppose it is intended they should. Don't cry, May dearest. We could not help it."

"If I were to go to our father, and tell him," said May, timidly.

"O no, May; certainly not. Robert would never forgive us. It would estrange him from us," added she eagerly, as if seeking for an argument to satisfy herself; "and that would never be right, for we should have no influence over him. Come, May, I know what you will like. Let us go into the elm-tree avenue, and tell our beads togeth.r;" and she drew her sister's arm into her own.

May yielded, but with a wistful look on her sweet face. The beads told, the sisters went into the house. Presently the great bell rang out for supper, and they descended. The Earl entered the supper-room. He was accompanied by a young man of some twenty-three or four years of age—a stranger to the girls.

"I must present your cousin to you," said the Earl; "Philip Engelby, by your leave."

The sisters made their reverence, and Philip bowed low.

"Where is Robert?" said Lord Edenhall, glancing round; "'tis ill manners, indeed, to keep us waiting. However, we will do without him. Philip, lead my daughter Rita to the table. May, you must honor me."

The Earl whispered to a servant, ere he sat down, to the effect that Viscount Milroy was to learn his presence in the supper-room was not required that evening.

"What makes you look so pale, May?" said her father, as, after the first dishes had been served, he had leisure to look round. May flushed crimson in a moment, and made no reply. An edict of total banishment from Mistress Dorothy's parlor was hovering on the Earl's lips, when his attention was attracted by the odd gestures of one of the old servants in attendance. "Morris," said he, "is anything amiss?" The man did not answer; but there was a sort of confused noise in the hall, the tramping of many feet.

Lord Edenhall started up, and threw the door open. A number of men were bearing something in their arms. Rita pressed forward, and uttered a cry of anguish. She turned to May, just in time to catch her ere she fell; and she lay senseless in her sister's arms.

CHAPTER II.

PHILIP'S PLANS.

T last that strange sort of lull that creeps over the house on which a heavy blow has fallen was felt at Edenhall. The body of the young heir, of the gallant, fearless boy, had been laid out for the grave. Massive wax candles burned in the room of death, and many of the women-servants were watching by the corpse. In a corner knelt Mistress Dorothy, the housekeeper; her sleeves hid the beads that were passing rapidly through her fingers as she prayed for the soul so suddenly summoned before its Judge. Unshriven he had passed, but not by his own fault.

Mrs. Dorothy was a person who, while perfectly maintaining her position as house-keeper, never preaching or obtruding her opinions, contrived to gain a wonderful influence over the minds of others. Perhaps her own serenity, or perhaps the constant prayer that bound her soul to God was the

secret. Be that as it may, Lord Milroy, who
would never listen to his sisters' remon-
strances, and defied his tutor as far as he
dared, had often held converse with Mrs.
Dorothy, had let her see into his heart; and
the memory of those glimpses gave her inex-
pressible comfort in this awful hour. With
confidence she could breathe the words of
Holy Church: "Remember not the sins of
his youth and his ignorance, for though he
hath sinned he hath not denied Thee."

The sisters had wept themselves to sleep;
the Earl was shut up in his chamber, for
none might look on the proud man's grief.
On the terrace, outside the hall, paced slowly
up and down Philip Engelby, his eyes fixed
on the distant horizon, where the faint flush
of early dawn might be descried.

"Strange chances of life," he mused; "in
an instant, from a poor dependent on a great
man's state to become heir-at-law; the one
great obstacle in my path swept away in a
moment. Is not my onward progress clear
and plain? 'Tis easy now to mount. Yet
he may wed again. I scarce think it. But
what boots the title without the lands?

What useless folly thus to divide the inheritance? There is but one remedy—to win the hand of one of these fair girls, and I trow few would murmur at that condition. I know not which is the fairer, the stately Rita or the dove-like May. Which would be the easier to win? As the proverb runs, I must look well to my cards. Methinks it would be seemly if I delivered them from my presence till the burying be over. I wonder of what sort is the parson, and whether he would give me lodging? I take it parsons are mostly hangers-on at great men's tables; and he will gladly pleasure the *heir-at-law*. I'll creep softly to my chamber now, and put together my effects; and when the sun has risen I will seek my fortune with Parson Hunter."

Philip was right in his judgment. When day brought back its miseries, when the mourners with aching nerves and downcast hearts came out to receive their guest, great was their satisfaction to find he had departed. The Earl especially appreciated the proceeding; Philip made a tremendous stride in his favor by the step. It showed a thoughtful-

ness for others, together with that frankness
which would not simulate a sorrow he could
not feel—all of which impressed Lord Edenhall favorably. His first impulse was to
hate the man who was now heir to the
family honors and name, and to determine
such brilliant prospects never should become
a reality; but this move of Philip's somewhat changed his mind. He was adverse to
marrying again. His heart was still, in a
strange sort of way, faithful to his lost wife.
Marriage with a young damsel would be
most distasteful to him. There was an old
prophecy—the Earl called it an old woman's
tale—that if ever the house of Edenhall
denied the faith, there should never more be
an heir in the direct line.

"Folly!" said the Earl to himself, as he
strode feverishly about the room: "I suppose the old cronies will be croaking over
my poor lad's grave with such stuff as this?
I suppose Providence had arranged the horse
was to throw him, and the fact of his
mounting it, when warned it was untrained,
is to count for nothing."

Still, notwithstanding this soliloquy, the

thought that even if he did re-enter the
uninviting state of matrimony, the curse
might yet be fulfilled, recurred with an
unpleasant frequency to his mind; and
before the day closed, following that which
saw the ending of Robert's young life, he had
been talking to Philip (who of course presented himself in the course of each day to
make inquiries) in a tone of friendly confidence, which raised high the hopes in the
young man's breast.

The following day fortune seemed to favor
him still further. Strolling about the
grounds, he came on Rita alone. She was
sitting in an attitude of the deepest dejec-
tion. A book which she had been trying to
read had fallen from her hands; the tears
were slowly coursing down her pale cheeks.

Very high-spirited people are generally
more utterly cast down by sorrow than those
more usually serene; and Rita felt the loss
of her joyous, handsome, mischievous, but
loving brother to her heart's core. She
colored up as she saw Philip, and bent her
head; she was feeling too languid and worn
out to rise.

"Pardon me, fair coz," he said, bending low, "if I disturb you; say but one word and I am instantly gone. But if you would suffer me to break in upon the sad train of your thoughts, not to jar against, but to harmonize with them, how blest I should esteem myself!"

"I shall be but dull company, cousin Philip," answered the girl, sadly; "I cannot school my spirits to play my part of hostess. Let me thank you, cousin, for taking up your abode with Parson Hunter. I fear your lodging is but a sorry one."

Philip smiled, and evaded the last question, but picked up the book lying on the ground.

"What! poetry, cousin? Do you study this? I am madly fond of it. Doubtless you know the Italian tongue, and have many a strain of Dante by heart?"

Rita answered she knew Italian well; and, standing before her, the young man began some of the immortal lines of the great master, which touched the sensitive heart of Rita and made it thrill.

It was like balm dropping on a wound.

Philip seated himself on the grass at her feet, and the conversation ran swiftly on. He learned her tastes, her favorite pursuits, the books she read, the heroes she delighted in. Proud and reserved as she naturally was, she would not have believed it possible an hour before that she could have talked so openly to a stranger; but with consummate tact he led her on. He possessed to the full the power of pleasing, and he exerted it to the utmost. She had been pining for action —to see the world—only now that this blow had come, she cared for naught. She wanted to do some great thing; she could not be content to spend her life spinning and embroidering, visiting poor people, and entertaining a few country neighbors.

"No," said Philip, with kindling light in his eyes, "you would say with the poet"— and he opened the volume of George Herbert she had been reading—

"The sure traveller,
Though he alight sometimes, still goeth on;
Write on the others—' Here lies such a one.' "

"Yes, that is just what I feel," said Rita, in a glow of delight at being so well understood.

She was ashamed the next minute at having seemed so to forget the sorrow of the present moment Philip saw he had said enough for one day, and presently after took his leave. But the sorrowful train of Rita's reflections had been broken; she was looking cheerful when May came to join her.

May had been praying in the chamber of death. It was not the first time in her young life that her devotion had kept her out of a snare. For the last twenty-four hours Philip's thoughts had been turning to her. There was a great attraction to him in the apparent yielding softness of her manner and character; but the lucky chance that threw him in Rita's way was not to be despised, and from henceforth his mind was resolved to win her.

When May joined her sister, Rita told her about Philip.

"I don't like him," said May, softly.

"For Heaven's sake, why?" rejoined Rita, fretfully. "You have such extraordinary fancies. His parts are excellent, his manners most agreeable."

"He is not true, I think," said May, slowly, and in a sorrowful tone.

"Well, really, sister, I wonder you do not scruple to burden your conscience. This man has never wronged you. You cannot know he is untrue. You can only guess it, and read it in his face, as you fancy. I think you lack charity, sister mine."

"It may be so, Rita, dearest," answered May, humbly; "perhaps it is wrong for me to see these things in faces. I have no one to ask now"—and her eyes filled with tears. "In Paris, dear Sœur Genevieve and Père de Lyonne used to teach me how to correct my faults. I will not do it again."

"Darling May," said Rita, as she kissed her fondly, "it was I that the good nun and priest had to torment them. You never had any faults."

"O Rita, hush!"

May's eyes were overflowing now, and the subject of Philip Engelby was for the moment forgotten.

CHAPTER III.

THE APOSTLE OF THE SACRED HEART.

T early dawn on the thirteenth of October, 1688, while the Thames was wrapped in a cold white mist, and little traffic had as yet begun to waken London from its slumbers, a solitary figure was seen lingering in the neighborhood of the Tower, and watching the disembarkation of the travellers from the bark *Clotilde*, which had come alongside the wharf hard by the grim old fortress. It was the figure of one tall and strongly built, with an open, fearless and resolute countenance, much sunburnt from frequent exposure to the weather.

When he saw a slight, tall gentleman, evidently a foreigner, leave the vessel and cast an inquiring glance about him, as if expecting some one to meet him, he advanced; and as soon as he was within earshot of the individual, he approached and uttered a few Latin words in a low tone. They were understood and responded to, and the passenger immediately turned to see after his luggage. This was, however, of such small dimensions that it was easily found, and soon shouldered by a lad who had also been loitering about, and was apparently known and trusted by the first comer.

The two gentlemen walked away together.

"Welcome to England," said the Englishmen, speaking in French; "welcome to the 'land of crosses,' my good father and brother in Christ."

"A thousand thanks," answered the other. "I have thanked God He had deemed me worthy to share in some part in your sufferings, Reverend Father. I doubt not that I speak to our Superior in London."

"Yes," returned the other, "I am that unworthy personage. owner of various holes and corners where sundry of ours abide, and Superior of certain men whose lives are in their hands, and whose whereabouts, sometimes for weeks together, are unknown to me. Yet, thanks to our good God, I think we are all true at heart, and as faithful to the counsels of our blessed Father as our straits will permit."

"I have known little, too little, of England," answered the other. "Occupied in the duties of my office as Superior of our residence at Paray-le-Mon'al, a poor little town in Burgundy doubtless your reverence has never heard of, I have contented myself with praying for those of ours whom I knew to be struggling in this battle-field, and you may imagine my surprise when the orders of my Provincial naming me as chaplain to the princess arrived. My stay in Paris was brief, and I have heard little; but I had deemed, father, that since the restoration of the monarchy your times had been more peaceful, and that even sanguine hopes were entertained that the Church should arise again in this isle."

"It is true, mon pere," said Father Whitbread. "In comparison of what we had to endure during the Commonwealth, and before it, we have had peace since his Majesty's accession. But the justice we looked for at his hands has been unhappily denied us. The great fire which reduced the larger part of this city to ashes some ten years ago was laid to our charge by popular prejudice, and since then an increasing dislike and animosity to us has been growing. I misdoubt me much whether we have not a fresh storm of persecution at hand. Stringent bills against us have been brought into Parliament, but have not as yet passed into law. Oppressive orders have been issued by the Privy Council, but have not as yet been put into force. We have need of extreme caution on the one hand, lest we should spoil all the good that has been done, and of extreme courage on the other, lest we should gain naught. You see," added he, with a smile, "you are in very deed entering the camp; there is no mistaking our enemy, and often have we to say with holy David, "*Dum appropiant super me nocentes ut edant carnes meas ; si consistant udversum me castra, non timebit cor meum, si exsurgat adversum me prœlium, in hoc ego sperabo.*"* And now if it please you, we must embark again; we will take boat unto Westminster. I am leading you to a house near there, where I

---

* "Whilst the wicked draw near against me to eat my flesh; if armies in camp should stand together against me, my heart shall not fear; if a battle should rise up against me, in this will I be confident."

have the *entrée.* I desire, and I am sure you will share my wish, to pass by our glorious abbey. To-day is the Feast of St. Edward the Confessor; and though we may not kneel at his shrine, we will gaze on the gray walls still sanctified by the presence of his holy remains."

A few boats plying for hire were lying by the river's bank. Into one of these the two gentlemen stepped, and were borne swiftly up the stream. The white mist was rolling away before the sun, and, as they neared Westminster, a flood of rosy light and golden beams were falling on the gray towers of the abbey, making it seem, for the moment, like a "house not made with hands." The boat neared the shore, the two passengers disembarked, and were soon standing beneath the shade of those mighty walls

"*Sancte Edwarde, ora pro nobis,*" murmured Father Whitbread.

"Amen," answered Père de la Colombière. "Most glorious Saint," he continued, in a low tone, "I place under thy protection my mission to the country thou didst so fondly love and so wisely govern. True servant of

our Master, whose tender charity towards
men was like unto His, the riches of whose
Divine Heart have begun to be made known
unto me, though so vile and so unworthy,
intercede for me, that I may fulfill the trust
He hath given me, and may kindle in this
poor country a more burning flame of His
Divine love."

There was a moment's silence, and the two
priests turned away. The prayer had mounted
up to heaven. The Apostle of the Sacred
Heart had set his foot on English ground,
and begun his work. Little recked the great
city, in which the din and turmoil of life
was now beginning to be heard, of this new
comer, of his prayer and of his mission.

By the vast majority, he would, if known
at all, be known only to be hated, by others
feared, by many scorned. And we who
think we would have knelt to kiss the hem
of his garment, and hang on the words that
fell from his lips, are chafed at their blind
folly and indifference, forgetting how far
back in the long centuries a Messenger in-
finitely greater, with more wondrous tidings
still, came in the darkness of the midnight

to a sleeping world, and, in silence and obscurity, through which no eye of man could pierce, took up His abode on earth, unknown and unadored, save by the astonished angels and the Virgin Mother.

CHAPTER IV.

LADY DIANA.

"GOOD morrow, Phil," cried Hugh Lindsay, tapping the person he addressed lightly on the shoulder. "It is time, I think, you should show yourself to the longing eyes of your friends. Why, man alive, who ever heard of such a piece of luck! A fine figure the future earl will cut at court now. What makes you look so glum?"

"Your folly," returned Philip Engelby, impatiently. "What difference does it make to me? I am but heir-at-law to the title and a beggarly estate, and those fine prospects may be snatched from me any day. My cousin is in the prime of life; he may wed again."

"Tush, man! the chances are against it. The bride the Earl woos is a place in the Privy Council. If he were to wed, he might have no sons, or they might be obliging enough to die in their cradles. Besides, of course, you are to be mated with one of the fair daughters. See if our friend Jonas doth not make it marvellously more easy to let you have his gold pieces than he doth to a poor dog like myself."

Philip smiled.

"That will be a good thing, at least, for I stand in great want of sundry gold angels at this very moment. But a truce to all this nonsense, Dick. Shall I find your sister, think you, if I go to pay my *devoirs* to her ladyship?"

Dick linked his arm within that of his friend as they walked down Birdcage Walk together.

"I suppose so; but, Phil, take my counsel for once—keep out of Diana's way."

A hot angry flush mounted to Philip's brow.

"Why?" asked he, sharply. "Is that a message from her to me?"

"Heaven help me, no," said Dick, with bitterness. "Di is only too glad to get you within her toils again; but no good can come of it, Phil. You have lost enough, suffered enough through her already. You have your fortune to make, and you have your foot now on the first round of the ladder. I'll not love to see Di's hands pull you down."

"I think, my good Dick," cried Philip, trying to put on an indifferent manner, "mourning over my long absence in the country hath turned your brain. Spare yourself the pains, my good fellow, of becoming mentor to your humble servant. I'd rather not climb any ladder if I am to be pushed up thereon by the kindly offices of my friends. I'll carve my own way, or, by my halidome, I'll leave it alone! Come, no more of this. Tell us the news. How goes it with the fair Duchess?"

"Very proud of her bantling, I believe," answered Dick, "and looking more lovely than ever since she hath come forth from her sick chamber. The Duke is ill content with Providence, it seems. He takes it as a sorry trick that a second time a daughter should have been dealt into his quiver. Time enough for seven sons to follow, I should say."

"Is the Queen more condescending towards

her highness since the infant hath been
born?" asked Philip.

"I trow not. Women have no mercy on
each other, thou knowest. Catharine hath
not forgottten the visit of last year."

"What folly!" said Philip, impatiently.
"Mary Beatrice was a child—is a child still,
for that matter—and how could she resist
the will of the Duke and the King?"

"I never said or thought she could, but
how will you convince the Queen? Her
Spanish blood is up; she thinks only that
the Tuscan has scorned her. She has no
pity for the helpless wife. They have sent
away her chaplain, too," continued Dick.
"St. Germain is gone—driven out of the
country by that fellow Luzancy, who, to my
certain knowledge, would swear away his
own mother's life if you gave him ten gold
angels for it. Why, even Du Marcsque, who
is as bitter against the Papists as man need
be, came forward to expose him, saying unto
me, 'If the King and his brother choose to
wed with Popish women, and agree they
shall have their idolatries in private, it
matters little which fanatic is in attendance

on them. It matters more that a rogue like
Luzancy should not go unpunished.'"

"And yet, you say, St. Germain is ban-
ished?"

"In truth I do," laughed Dick, "and
more besides. What think you but my
Lord of London hath taken him by the
hand, hath sent him to Oxford, and meaneth
in good earnest to induct him to a living?
Faugh! the heat these men display, on the
one hand, and the idolatry of the Papists,
on the other, make me sick of all religion."

"And is no one to replace St. Germain?"

"'Tis said one is even now on his way, a
favorite of the most puissant Louis; he hath
not yet arrived, as far as I know. But here
we are at the palace gates. If you are going
in, we must part, for I must go and hunt up
old Jonas; and he dwelleth now hard by
the abbey, just for all the world like the
old gnomes and ghouls they carve outside
the abbey door."

Philip laughed, and the friends parted—
Dick Lindsay sauntering off towards the
Abbey of Westminster, whose glorious gray
towers stood out in sharp outline against

the blue sky; and Philip wending his way
amidst the winding passages and staircases
of St. James' Palace. After many inquiries,
he found the apartments of the "governess
of the royal children," and was at length
ushered by a lackey into her presence.

Lady Diana Villiers was a tall, stately
person; her sallow complexion and in-
differently formed features were redeemed
by her immense lustrous black eyes. When
those eyes were cast down, and the features
were in repose, she looked plain, if not posi-
tively ugly; but, when her eyes, sparkling
with light, were turned on any one—when
her face grew animated, and her wondrous
power of pleasing was brought into play—
there were few women more fascinating.

"Welcome, Philip," said she, as Engelby
entered, and bowed profoundly before her.
"I suppose you have come to inquire after
the welfare of your fair cousins."

"Will not your ladyship give me credit
for wishing to know how it fares with yourself?" said Philip, in an aggrieved tone.

Lady Diana laughed.

"No; I fancy I should not have been

honored with this visit if Lord Edenhall's
aaughters were not at court. Be seated,
Philip, I beg of you;" and she waved him
towards a seat. "The two Marguerites are
appointed maids of honor to the Duchess,
and a very pretty addition they will be to
our ducal court. For your sake I shall
watch over them, if in any way I can serve
them. 'Tis pity they be Papists."

Philip's eyes had been fixed on the ground
while Lady Diana was speaking. He now
glanced keenly up at her face: a mocking
smile sat on his lips.

"And what are your plans for the future,
Philip? In what way doth the decease of
this poor lad affect you?"

"I hardly know," answered he, "as yet.
My cousin hath shown great friendliness
towards me, and hath promised to use his
influence to obtain me a place as secretary
to one of the cabinet. I am to wait on him
to day to learn my fate. The future is all
uncertain."

"But fair to view," replied Lady Diana;
"methinks I can read the lines, though I
am no fortune-teller. Rely on me that I

wil. do all in my power to further your
cause. Your interests shall be ever dear to
me, Philip, though doubtless you have
thought otherwise."

The young man's lips quivered, and his
eyes flashed.

"What will an earldom and all the world
be to me, Di, without you? With you, I
could have won my way to fortune. Without you, I strive and scheme at times, but
the game is not worth the trouble."

Lady Diana rose to her feet.

"Philip, there must be an end to this.
If you choose to refer to the past of our careless, thoughtless youth, all intercourse
between us must cease. I do not regret my
step. Romantic poverty is well for ballads
and tales, but not for real life, I trow. Forget that we have ever been more than companions in childhood and friends in youth,
a: d you shall have no surer friendship than
mine; if you choose to *remember*, all is over
between us."

She waved her hand, and Philip, with a
sullen look, advanced towards the door.
Her voice arrested him on the threshold.

"Be wise, Philip, and do not throw away my friendship. I bid you in the name of the Duchess to her next reception; let us meet there as friends. Be a man, Philip, and do not kick away the ball when it lies at your feet."

Philip bowed low, and left the room. He could not trust himself to speak. He hastened out of the palace, and into the park of St. James, walking quickly, with his hat drawn over his brows, while he struggled and fought with conflicting emotions.

"Be it so," said he, at last; "let her work her will. Here at her bidding I cast aside the last shred of what she calls romance. I was a fool. The sight of her unmanned me. It brought back too strong a memory of the days when, troth-plighted, we wandered together in the glades near her Scottish home. She spoke not so bitterly of *Papists* then. Alack, time brings its changes! Why pine I for her heart? Tush, she hath no heart to give! I'll follow her example, throw my folly to the winds, forget the old lessons of truth and honor we learned together, and climb, as best I may, that ladder poor Dick spoke of anon. Hark, the abbey chimes the hour! It is time and enough for me to present myself to my uncle's house."

And so saying, Philip settled his hat in the fashionable style for young men of the day, and went his way to Lord Edenhali's house in Pall Mall.

CHAPTER V.

STRUGGLE AND DEFEAT.

THE long suite of reception rooms in St. James' Palace were brilliantly lighted up and filled with a gay company. In one of them card-tables were arranged, and some devoted lovers of the pastime were eagerly making up their sets and longing for the time when the etiquette of the court would allow them to begin.

As yet, however, both Duke and Duchess were on their feet: James, engaged in conversation with a knot of gentlemen; Mary Beatrice, receiving her guests, as one after another they passed before her to make their abeisance and accept a few pleasant words from her charming lips. Her lithe graceful form was attired in a robe of blue satin, while her beautiful raven hair was dressed in a mass of curls, built up on her head in a structure at least not more unbecoming than some of our modern fashions. One

long curl was suffered to stay on each side
of her neck. Her sweet face was lit up with
smiles; for not only was she at all times a
gracious princess, but the joy that she felt
in again becoming a mother, after the loss
of her first baby in the preceding year, danced
in her eyes, and rang in the tones of her voice.
It was her first reception since her recovery,
and the room was filled with guests, hasten-
ing to pay their congratulations to the
Duchess, and inquire after the welfare of
the infant Princess Isabella. It was a
strange medley which thus thronged the
rooms. Some of the worst and best of London society at that period—some who, save
at a formal levée, would never enter Whitehall, loved to pay homage to the gentle
Duchess; some who, anxious always to trim
their sails, saw in the Duke the heir pre-
sumptive to the crown; others who admire d
his prowess as Lord High Admiral; and
others who came no one exactly knew why.

Near the Duchess stood her two newly
appointed maids of honor, dressed alike, and
both looking very lovely. The exitement
had flushed Rita's cheek, while timidity made

May somewhat pale. The former was beginning to use her great Spanish fan (then first
brought into vogue by the Queen, and the
rage among ladies) in the way she saw those
around her do. May gladly sheltered
herself behind its immense folds, and gazed
on at the novel scene with wondering eyes.

Our readers may think it strangely in-
consistent of Lord Edenhall to have placed
his daughters in the ducal court. The Earl
was a curious compound. He had brought
them to town, intending to seek places for
them in the Queen's household; but the
unfeigned horror of May, when the real history of the debased court of Charles II was
made known to her, arrested him. When,
with streaming eyes and trembling form, his
gentle, yielding child threw herself at his
feet, and implored him to save her from
such misery, he seemed to see before him
the lost wife whose every wish had been his
law; and, in truth, that very night, after he
had driven May sternly away, the shadowy
form of that wife seemed to stand by his bedside, and warn him that no harm should
come to the pearls she had left in his keep-

ing. With morning light, the Earl jeered at himself for his folly; but, before the day was over, he had sought and cbtained places for his girls in the household of the Duchess of York.

"I am charmed to see you, my Lord Stafford," said the Duchess, as a stately, gray-headed old nobleman bowed low before her, "and your fair daughters also. It is long since I have seen you, Lady Alethea. I trust you have not been sick. You look pale; but I need not ask the question of Lady Katherine, for she is blooming like a summer rose."

And, when the Ladies Howard had replied, the Duchess turned to May.

"Come hither, my English dove," said she; "here are companions with whom, if I mistake not, you will like to keep company. Take her, Lady Alethea, under your wing, or, I doubt not, she will sit in a corner the whole evening, gazing at us with her wistful eyes. And make acquaintance also with my other Margaret."

And, with a smile, the Duchess moved on to greet another party.

The two sets of sisters speedily made
friends; and, as the reception was now over,
and the guests began to amuse themselves,
Rita and Kate Howard strolled away together,
while May and Alethea sat chatting in a quiet
corner. Whilst laughing at some innocent
joke, a shadow fell across them, and May
was accosted by Philip Engelby. Philip, in
court dress, with his curled and perfumed
peruke covering his head and shoulders,
looked so different from the plainly attired
gentleman who had been her father's guest
at Edenhall that, for a moment, she looked
at him in surprise; then, coloring prettily,
begged his pardon, and introduced him to
her companion.

He asked for Rita, and May pointed her
out to him at no great distance; and, to her
intense relief, after paying the two girls a
few of the high flown compliments then the
custom in society, he moved towards Marguerite.

"You do not look as if you much favored
your cousin, Lady Margery," said Alethea,
slyly.

"I fear I don't," replied May, blushing.

"Rita thinks me unjust; and, indeed, I know so few people, and so little of the world, as she says, that it is rash to form a judgment."

"I have never seen him before," said Alethea; "the lines of his face are hard; but, if all be true that the world hath said of him and Lady Di Villiers, he is much to be pitied."

"Oh," said May, shrinking back, "there it is again! I do not like Lady Diana, and it seems so wrong, for she has loaded us with kindness ever since we came into the household. I do not know why it is," continued May, looking up into Alethea's face, "that I say all this to you, but I feel as if we were going to be fast friends."

"So we are," answered the other, brightly; "and, in these days, all Catholics should stand by each other, and be true to each other, even in the smallest things. I will tell you about your cousin, Margery; for, perhaps, 'tis as well you should know it. But tell me first, has the new Chaplain to the Duchess arrived? I am sure no one can hear us. They are all going to cards, or busy talking, far from us. I want to know. We regretted Père St. Germain so much."

"He came two days ago," replied May; "he had his first audience with the Duchess to-day. I only saw him for a moment; for Lady Diana was in attendance on her Highness, and it was only a formal audience to present the greetings of the King of France to the Duchess. He has the aspect of a most spiritual mortified man."

"Such is his reputation," Alethea said.

"Father Harcourt is charmed with him, and says London hath a treasure. Alas! poor London will reck little of him. But I trust that we who may have access to him will profit by it."

"Well, now, of your cousin, May. I suppose you know your exact relationship to him?"

"My Aunt Dora, who married Colonel Engelby, of Mortwood, had one son, I was told. Both his parents died while he was a child, and he was brought up with my father and uncles. But, when the civil war broke out, he espoused the cause of the Parliament, married the daughter of a Roundhead, and brought up his son in the same principles. I know he and his wife are dead; and now Philip is loyal to the King."

"So far true, sweet May; but perhaps you know not that Philip was the owner of goodly estates under the Commonwealth, but lost them all at the Restoration. He was betrothed to Lady Diana Lindsay, who had no fortune. When she found he had become poor, and would have to carve his way to fortune, she threw him over, and married Sir David Villiers, old enough to be her father. Sir David has been holding a post of honor at the Hague. So it is only a year ago since Lady Diana appeared in London, and the King appointed her governess to the royal children. She was a Catholic in those days, and, 'tis said, had she married Philip, he would have gone back to the faith of his ancestors."

"Poor fellow!" said May, compassionately. "No wonder his face is hard. No doubt Rita knows this tale, and has pitied him. I will try and judge him less harshly, and Lady Diana, too. Let us pray for her. Oh, how could she renounce the faith! Now you have told me this, I remember the strange light in her face when Père de la Colombière was ushered in to-day. Perchance that good father will bring her back."

"Hush!" said Alethea, who, while talking, had her eyes constantly looking about. "She comes this way."

Lady Diana swept by. She was magnificently dressed, and looked exceedingly haughty. She had thrown a large and costly shawl about her.

"Good evening, young ladies," she said. "Swearing eternal friendship, I see. All the world is busy. I must go and see how my little Princess fares."

And she passed on. She had been the centre of a group, attracted by her sparkling wit and stately presence. For a while Philip Engelby had lingered on its outskirts, but had soon detached himself, and wandered to the side of Marguerite. There he had settled down, and was evidently making the time pass pleasantly, to judge from the bursts of merry laughter he elicited from Rita and Kate Howard. Lady Diana watched them, and grew pale. She laughed and jested on; and then, rising, dismissed her group, with an assertion that she must go and visit the

royal nursery; and, as we have seen, she
hastened from the room.   When Lady Diana
gained the corridors which led to her own
apartment, she stood still; she was in perfect
solitude.   The occupants of the different
rooms were gone to the reception; the servants were busy in other parts of the palace.
It was one of those rare moments of freedom
from observation in the life of a court official.
What a change came over the face but lately
smiling and gay!   What a look of haggard
grief, of hopeless sorrow!   She pressed her
hands to her brow, as if to still the pain.
"Can I, dare I go?" she whispered to herself.   "Am I mad?   I have gone too far to
recede now.   What folly to recur to the
past!   Yet there is somewhat in that man's
aspect that draws me on.   There is a strange
yearning in my soul to speak with him.   I
must do it."

She suddenly opened with a key an *armoire*
let into the wall of the corridor, took from
it a large gray cloak, and, throwing it over
her so completely as to conceal both face
and figure, went with rapid steps into another
part of the palace.   She met no one.   The

place was deserted. She ascended more than one staircase, and traversed many a corridor. At last she stopped before a closed door and knocked. A voice within, speaking in French, bade her enter. She did so, shutting the door behind her, and found herself in the presence of Père de la Colombière. Two small rooms had been assigned for his use, and he had already rendered them as plain and simple in appearance as possible. The outer room opened into the private chapel of the Duchess, for, contrary to the articles of her marriage convention, Mary Beatrice was not allowed to use the Royal Chapel of St. James.

The father was seated at his writing-table, and rose as the veiled lady entered. Already aware that his counsel would generally be sought in secret, he was not surprised at the apparition. He opened the door which led into the sanctuary, and the soft light of the lamp cast in its rays. Then, when he had seated himself in his confessional, Lady Diana knelt beside him. Her whole frame shook with emotion, and it was some moments before she could speak. Gradually she told

her story. She had abjured her faith for
the sake of this world's gauds, and a cease-
less remorse consumed her. Power, influence, riches, were hers; they sickened her as
she grasped them. With burning jealousy
she beheld Philip, whom she had wronged
and renounced, devote himself to win Marguerite's favor. Her soul was torn by
passion, and the powers of good and evil
were fiercely contending within her.

At first all the stores of Father de la
Colombière's compassion were poured out on
her. He spoke, with an eloquence she had
never heard before, of the sweetness of penance, the fulness of pardon. But as the
conversation went on, his patience was sorely
tried. It was but a wild impulse that had
brought her to his feet. She wanted peace,
but she would not pay its price. She would
give up naught of the power she held; she
would neither declare her faith in public,
nor even seek to practice it in private. When
her excess of grief and passion was over she
grew calm; and if the father could have seen
her face he would have found it hardened
again to play her part. Words of stern

remonstrance rose to his lips, but they were
not uttered. He looked at the quivering
lamp, and the memory of his special mission
given him by his Master came strongly into
his soul. With words of deepest tenderness
he spoke on:

"My poor child," he said, "if you still
wander from the fold the Good Shepherd
will pursue you with unfailing love. No
words can speak the tenderness of His heart.
His love shall follow you into all the scenes
of pleasure and pomp you cannot forego.
Wander as you will, you cannot escape from
that undying love."

"I must not tarry longer," said Lady
Diana, rising to her feet. "Pardon, father,
that I have troubled you. 'Twas a phantom
of my brain. I have gone too far now to
recede. Persecution is not to my taste."

"Come back to me again," said the priest.
"Look on me as a friend; for surely in the
turmoil of your restless life you need one."

"No," said Lady Diana, in a cold, hard
voice. "I have been forced to come this
once, but I will no more. You might attain
a power over me I could not resist. I have
made my choice, and I will abide by it."

She was gone, and Père de la Colombière, kneeling before the tabernacle, asked for light and grace to bring back to the fold this soul and the many others who had been led astray by the glare of this world's honor and the fear of this world's frown.

CHAPTER VI.

THE HIDDEN NUNS.

IT was a bright sunshiny morning on the 8th of December, 1676. There had been a hard frost for some days preceeding its advent, but now the sunbeams sparkled on the ice-bound trees and frosty grass in the Park of St. James, and made them glitter with silver brightness.

It was very early, so much so that few persons were on foot, when the lumbering coach of "my Lord Stafford" stopped at the door of Lord Edenhall's house in Pall Mall; and though the housemaids of those days would have been astonished to find themselves in bed even two hours before its arrival, yet even they wondered why Lady Alethea Howard and their own Lady Margery should choose to be carried to Kensington at such an exceedingly early hour. However, there the two noble damsels were, looking blithe and gay, as they climbed into

the grand coach we should now so heartily
despise. Large woolen cloaks with hoods
both served to keep them warm and to
shelter them from observation. Each lady
carried a mask in her hand, for masks were
then in high vogue, and Catholics often
found the fashion a very useful one. The
coach rolled off with its two inmates, the
driver directed his horses up the Long street
(now known as that of St. James) into
"Piccadilly," then a broad country road,
with here and there the detached mansion
of some great personage. Various lanes
branched off from the main road. At the
corner of one of these stood an alehouse bearing the sign of the Half Moon, and up this
lane the coach turned; before it had gone
far it stopped.

A staid elderly man who had been sitting
by the driver descended and assisted the
ladies to alight. Both of them were now
masked, and, following the servant, they set
out on foot. Indeed, nothing save the
roughest cart could have passed over the
ground they now traversed; they soon came
out on an open space of grass called May

Fair—the scene of much noisy revelry in May and the succeeding summer months, but which in winter time was utterly forsaken. Turning to the right, the maidens ascended some rising ground, treading their way through clumps of trees, now and again getting entangled in tufts of brushwood. At length, on reaching the top of the little hill we have spoken of, they came to a farm-yard, in the midst of which rose a homely two-storied grange or farm with a thatched roof.

It was larger than it seemed, for the trees growing close around hid its double roof. In the yard, leaning on a p'gsty, was a man of middle age, belonging, if we might judge from his dress, to the laboring class, with a spade over his shoulder. He turned round at the sound of footsteps, and looked keenly at the party; but Alethea approaching him unmasked, the farmer bowed low.

"Good-morrow, Master Lyde," said she; "are we in time?"

"Yes, my young lady, in good time; for no one else hath yet arrived. Hasten on, and you will be made welcome. And you, my trusty Richard," added he, nodding to the

man-servant, "come, tell me how you think
my pigs are looking."

Alethea, followed by May, lifted the latch
of the door, and walked into the homely
kitchen. A woman was standing at the fire
settling various pots and pans.

"Dearest Magdalene," said Alethea, and
the two friends embraced. Magdalene Lacy
was dressed exactly as beseemed a farm-
servant. Her kirtle and jacket were both of
some coarse gray material, and protected by
a check apron, while a mob-cap hid her hair,
and was gathered by a string close round her
face. But one look at that face told May she
was no farmhouse cookmaid.

The delicately marked features, the white
forehead, and the air of refinement about her,
spoke of gentle birth.

"You see," said Magdalene, with a smile,
after she had greeted May, "it is my turn in
the kitchen this week. You are in good
time, dear Alethea. I think I may leave my
pots now, and take you upstairs."

So saying, she led the way to the adjoining
room—a sort of scullery, in one corner of
which was a ladder that led up to the floor
above.

"Now, May, you must learn to climb," said Alethea, gaily. "This is Jacob's ladder," and she began nimbly to mount it.

May followed, and they found themselves in a large low room under the roof. Its usual furniture was carefully packed away in one corner, and anything in the house which could be made into any sort of seat had been gathered together. The cross beams of the roof made the room look a little like a church, and the simple altar raised at one end told that such was indeed its temporary destination.

There were about six or seven persons in the room, all dressed in the same sort of manner as Magdalene, and all kneeling in prayer.

In a few minutes, Father Whitbread and Father de la Colombière entered the room. The former immediately vested for Mass, assisted by the latter. By the time the priest was ready, person after person came into the room. Master Lyde, and Richard, Lord Stafford's man, remained below to keep guard. The congregation seemed to have sprung out of the ground, and, of the fifty

or sixty persons who contrived to pack themselves into the narrow space, there was not
one who had not braved some danger or gone
through some difficulty to be present, and,
during the Holy Sacrifice, there was not a
wandering glance nor a single stifled yawn.

A large number of persons received Holy
Communion, and, at the close of the Mass, a
number of voices in admirable harmony
softly chanted the "*O Maria, sine labe con-
cepta;*" then, after a short pause, Père de la
Colombière turned to address the people.
Fortunately, we are not left to imagine what
were the words that fell from his lips. That
treasure has been preserved to us; and if,
even as we read the quaint old badly printed
French, our hearts are stirred within us, what
must have been the effect on those who
listened to his eloquence? "*Tota pulchra es,
amica mea, et macula non est in te,*"* echoed
through the room.

"You are not ignorant," said the
preacher, "of the noise that the arguments on the subject of the Immaculate

* "Thou art all fair, O my love, and there is not a spot
in Thee."

Conception of the Blessed Virgin have
made in the Church. Some doctors,
enlightened on other points, and true
Catholics, have believed that Mary was
not exempted from the curse incurred by all
the children of Adam; but so strong was the
opposite opinion that for many years, from
the schools and the chairs of professors,
arguments have poured forth in favor of the
Immaculate Virgin. All the universities of
Italy, Spain, France and Germany have
loudly maintained this doctrine; the acade-
mies have been closed against anyone who
would not bind himself by an oath to teach
that she has received the singular privilege
of being conceived without sin. Even the
princes of the earth have interested themselves in the cause of the Queen of Heaven,
and employed their authority in her defence.
Never on any subject have there been more
discourses, more conferences, or more dis-
putes; never have so many books been
written as on this matter. Finally, the
Vicar of Jesus Christ has spoken, and has
shut the mouths of all those whose opinions
were not sufficiently in favor of the sanctity

of our holy Mother. The whole universe hath looked on this judgment as an important victory,' as a triumph. Those who differed from us now agree, and at the present moment all is calm, all are united in the same belief. Incomparable advantage of recognizing a sovereign judge! Questions are decided, the repose of our people is not troubled by divers winds of doctrine. All minds and all hearts are in unison, and no opinion contrary to the honor of God or His saints can be established in the Church of Jesus Christ." *

* Père de la Colombière here refers to the Bull of Alexander Seventh, *Solicitudo omnium Ecclesiarum*, December 8th, 1661. In this Bull the Sovereign Pontiff says that Paul V had forbidden any public teaching of any opinion contrary to the doctrine of the Immaculate Conception, and Gregory XV extended this prohibition to private discourses. He himself renews this prohibition under more stringent penalties.

The patient caution of Holy Church ere she proclaims a dogma of faith is sufficiently seen by the fact that she allowed nearly two centuries to elapse after this decision (which Père de la Colombière believed to be final) before its actual definition.

The sermon which we quote was preached before the Duchess of York in St. James' Palace in December, 1676. We have only used our privilege in transposing the *place* in which the words were uttered.

Thus spoke the holy Jesuit two centuries ago of the doctrines so often in these days called modern inventions—the Immaculate Conception and the Papal Infallibility.

We have not space to give further details of the admirable sermon; its gist was to show his hearers the horror that God has of the smallest sin, since He ordained that the Mother of His Son should be exempted from its faintest involuntary stain.

After the service the congregation rapidly dispersed. Most of its members had come from long distances, and all were anxious to evade observation by getting to their homes as early as possible. Alethea and May, however, lingered, and when the altar had been removed, and all its funiture carefully packed away in secure hiding-places, a table was spread with a homely breakfast for the two priests and the guests.

CHAPTER VII.

THE NEW FESTA.

AY was now introduced to the seven companions of Magdalene Lacy. "Behold," said Alethea, as she presented her, "behold our English nuns of the Immaculate Conception, and you, Sisters, make acquaintance with a child of the Visitation."

"Are you nuns, indeed?" said May, wonderingly, as she looked at the group in their coarse secular garments, and then around at the rude loft which served them in turns for chapel, community-room and dormitory. Her thoughts had flown back to the beautiful and spacious church, the vast *salles*, the wide corridors, the pleasant cells of the great Visitation Convent in the Faubòrg St. Jacques.

"I trust so," answered Elizabeth Timperly, the Superior; "though we cannot wear our habit, nor have the beauty of conventual life as our Sisters do in Paris, yet I hope we keep our rule, and, what is more, the great rule for us all—to follow our Master in the way of the Cross."

"You are, I understand, a branch of the Order in the Faubourg St. Antoine," said Père de la Colombière. "I said Mass there on my way through Paris, and I promised your Superior, if it were in my power, to pay a visit to her 'hidden nuns' in London. I told her," added the Father, with the sunny smile which so often lit up his face, "that I should expect to find you 'hidden saints' also."

"They are good children enough, as times go," interrupted Father Whitbread; "but don't turn their heads, mon Père—they have a pretty hard work before them. It is all very well to be sitting here eating this frumenty (the quality of which, by the way, Sister Magdalene, shows you are a true Lincolnshire woman), but I want to know how we shall comport ourselves in Newgate, with no one to speak to but a toad staring at us, and—"

The peal of laughter that rang through the room stopped the good Father's flow of words, and obliged him to go on eating his frumenty, shaking his head over it with a woe-begone expression which he had put on for the occasion.

"You will frighten no one but Lady Margery, Father," said Alethea, when she could speak; "she has a mortal horror of toads; she actually ran away from one in our garden at Kensington, but I don't think an army of them would terrify our good Sisters."

"Father Rector takes a gloomy view of matters," observed Père de la Colombière. "I have been too short a time in the country to judge, and therefore, when I say things do not look so black to me, my words count for nothing."

"1 am not so sure of that," answered Father Whitbread; "but we did not come here to talk politics. Your visit here, mon Père, is a treat. I have promised these children, who, as I tell your reverence, are not as bad as they might be. I have promised them that you would speak to them on the devotion of which you told our Fathers at the conference you gave us, and the thought of which seemed to occupy you much. I

told these Sisters of it, and, of course, I have
had no peace since, till I consented to bring
you that they might hear it also."

"Yes, Sisters," said the Father, "I would
it were given to me to wake up in your souls
a devotion to the Sacred Heart of Jesus. It
would seem that it is the will of our Divine
Lord that a greater love to His Sacred
Humanity should be evinced by faithful
souls. You know, for you have been wisely
taught, that we should pay little heed to
visions, apparitions, and such like manifesta-
tions. Often they come from our own weak
imagination—or perchance from the enemy.
At all times they are not worth so much as a
single act of blind obedience, a single exer-
cise of heroic charity. It was, therefore,
with considerable distrust that, after my
appointment as Superior to our residence
in Paray-le-Monial, I consented, when asked
by the Superior of the Visitation Nuns, to
examine into the case of one of her religious,
who was either greatly favored by our Lord
or greatly deluded.

"I examined with all the care and prudence possible, and I was forced to conclude

the work was indeed of God, and that to this simple nun a mighty mission hath been given. I examined into her life, for hath not our Lord said, "by their fruits ye shall know them'? I found her childlike in obedience, grounded in humility, rooted in charity, and thirsting after sufferings.

"She hath gone through many trials, for in no Order is the slightest innovation on established customs so likely to be resisted as in the Visitation of Sainte Marie. It is yet in the full vigor of its early youth (may God send it shall never decay!), and the spirit of the blessed Bishop of Geneva and of the saintly Madame de Chantal was ever for a simple observance of the rule and customs. That a nun of this Order should have been chosen to make known this devotion is in itself a proof of its divine origin. As said Gamaliel of old, 'if this work be of men, it will come to nought; but if it be of God, you cannot overthrow it.' The Superior of the convent, also, is a person of singular prudence and holiness, and she fully believes that this holy soul is closely united to our Lord. The Mère de Saumaise was one of those who not only knew the sainted foundress of the Visitation, but was specially noticed by her as possessing rare gifts."

"May we know the name of this holy religious, Father?" said Mother Elizabeth Timperly.

"She is called Sister Margaret Mary in her convent," answered he; "I believe her family name is Alacoque. The first time that I visited the community to give a conference I was struck by her appearance. It is impossible to describe in what that impression consisted, save that I was convinced God would work great things by means of this soul. When, a little later on, the direction of her soul was committed to me, I had greater reason still for my conviction. I verily believe that our good and gentle Lord hath chosen Sister Margaret Mary to make known His will to us. Last year, during the Octave of Corpus Christi, she was in prayer before the tabernacle when our Lord appeared to her and showed her His Divine Heart. 'See this heart,' He said, 'which has loved men so much, and in return I receive from the greater part only ingratitude.' And then He said (and O, my Sisters, would that I could engrave these words in your hearts!), 'But what I feel still more is that there are hearts consecrated to Me that use Me thus.'"

He paused, overpowered by strong emotion, and some of his auditors were already in tears.

"Our Lord," continued the Father, "then condescended to ask of His servant to stir up the faithful to put aside the Friday after the Octave of Corpus Christi as an especial Feast to honor His Heart by communicating, and making a solemn act of reparation to atone for the indignities It receives while exposed on the altar. And then those Divine lips deigned to promise that His Sacred Heart should expand Itself to shed in abundance the influence of Its Divine love upon those who shall pay It this honor and procure it to be paid. Afterwards our merciful Lord told Sister Margaret Mary to bid my unworthy self do all in my power to establish this devotion and to give this pleasure to His Divine Heart. Dear Sisters, believing fully that this message was divine, I hastened

to obey it; and consecrated myself to the
Sacred Heart of Jesus on the Friday after
the Octave of Corpus Christi, which last
year fell on June the 21st—which is now
the Feast of Blessed Aloysius Gonzaga of our
Company—and my most earnest desire is to
wake up in the hearts of all, but especially
in those of religious men and women, an
ardent devotion to this Heart which has so
loved us. Ponder, dear Sisters, over my
words, and let them sink into your souls."

"We will, Father," answered Elizabeth
Timperly, as the Father rose; "but you will
visit us again, will you not? You will tell
us more of this holy Sister Margaret, and
teach us more fully how we can correspond
with the desires of our Blessed Master."

"I will, if it be possible to me," replied
Père de la Colombière; "but I trust before
long to be able to enter upon my thirty days'
retreat. I have told my royal mistress of my
desire, and I believe she will permit me to
be absent from her service for that space of
time. I count, my Sisters, on your prayers
for me." And then, after he had given his
blessing, Père de la Colombière began to

descend the ladder which led to the floor below.

Father Whitbread lingered behind for a moment.

"Do I not deserve prayers for bringing him?" he asked.

"You do, Father," returned the Superior, "and if it be possible for us to pray more for you than we do, you shall have more."

"I will send him to you when I can," he rejoined. "Value him you well; he is a rare gift that God hath lent to England for a while. If she, in her blindness, rejects him, let *us*, at least, profit by it, and put this treasure to good account." And bidding them farewell, he also disappeared.

CHAPTER VIII.

THE ROYAL CHAPEL.

OUR story has already shown that the friendship between Alethea Howard and Margery Clyme had grown apace. Lady Margery had not been long at court, and yet she was already learning a bitter lesson. As fresh flowers wither and fade in a heated atmosphere, so the flowers of the tender mutual love between herself and Marguerite had faded beneath the scorching glare of the world's ways and the world's pleasures.

Until the sisters came to London they had been as one. Always differing greatly in character, their deep love for each other had stood in the place of sympathy. And it was not the mere round of vulgar pleasures that had separated them now. Marguerite had plenty of admiration, and crowds of suitors would have been at her feet had she given them any encouragement. But she was absorbed in her affection and admiration of

Lady Diana. A young girl's friendship for a woman older than herself, and apparently her superior, is rare; but, when it occurs, the affection generally takes the form of a sort of idolatry. Thus it was with Marguerite. She was completely fascinated by the royal governess, who, on her side, did her best to throw her toils around her victim, and thus carry out her own ends. At this moment, those ends were not very clear to Lady Diana herself. She was so swayed by passion that her purpose changed day by day. At one time, she wished the marriage of Philip and Marguerite to take place, at others, the thought of it was abhorrent to her. For the most part, she contented herself with basking in the sunshine of Marguerite's adulation, and thus solacing herself for her domestic troubles. For Sir David Villiers had rapidly grown aged. He had been a hale old man for many years, but suddenly a trifling ailment had caused a break-up, and the once active politician had shrunk into a peevish invalid, peremptorily demanding his wife's attendance on him. Nor could she escape often under plea of

her duties; for not only was the Princess
Isabella a baby in arms, but the Duchess
of York was a fond and devoted mother, and
spent as much time as stern etiquette would
permit with her child. Therefore, Marguerite, who would wait patiently like a dog
in the ante-room for the flying visits or
chance moments Lady Diana could spare,
who would perform any commission, and
lavish any amount of sympathy, was the
delight of Lady Diana's eyes. May had
found herself totally neglected by her sister;
and, had it not been for Alethea, she would
have been lonely indeed.

One day, Dick Lindsay had come to call
on his sister and her husband, an occupation
of which he was not over fond. Lady Diana
was in some dismay—a person for whom she
had secured a place in the Duchess' private
chapel was unable to come.

"Her Highness will think it strange," she
cried, "to see the place I demanded vacant."

Dick, half in joke, offered to fill it, and
was taken at his word.

Places in the Duchess' private chapel were
eagerly sought for, for not only was the fame

of Père de la Colombière beg:nning to spread, but this chapel was the only one which might be resorted to without at least some fear of arrest.

Père de la Colombière, writing in November, 1676, from London to a friend in France, says: "The subjects of the King of England are not allowed to hear Mass in the Ambassadors chapels; and, since I have been here, people have been posted at the doors of all the chapels, even that of the Queen, to seize on the English they may see going out."

The chapel used by Mary Beatrice was, as we have mentioned before, not the royal chapel of St. James, but one of the Duchess' private apartments set apart for the purpose, and communicating with the dwelling-rooms of the chaplain.

Dick knew, therefore, he ran no risk by his appearance, and he went to the chapel with some curiosity. The Father gave a powerful discourse that day, but his words were lost on Dick. His place happened to be nearly opposite to that occupied by May and her sister, and having once fixed his eyes on May, Dick could think of nothing else.

She was unconscious of the notice she attracted, and when either wrapt in earnest devotion, or paying the deepest attention to the words of the preacher, she seemed to Dick as one too fair and spiritual to be a dweller on this earth.

There were the elements of a noble character in Dick Lindsay. He had been brought up to "conform to the times," and his ideas of religion altogether were very hazy. He had no fixed employments, but hung about the court in the manner of many young men of that day, and of all subsequent "days" and courts, waiting for some plum to fall into his mouth, and meanwhile wasting his little patrimony on dress and cards. To do Dick justice, he had stood the test of the corrupt atmosphere in which he lived marvellously well. Folly and idleness, rather than actual vice, had been his characteristics, and the first real affection he had ever felt seemed in an instant to ennoble his mind. He was not found that afternoon among the idlers on the Mall, who were accustomed to strut up and down showing off their gay apparel, for all the world like so many popinjays, and discussing the last bit of scandal with appetite.

Dick betook himself for a long solitary walk in the direction of Kensington. He had an extraordinary and sudden desire to know whereabouts stood Lord Stafford's house; for he now bethought himself that he had heard Philip Engelby say Lord Edenhall's younger daughter spent most of her time, when off duty, at this residence of the Stafford family.

CHAPTER IX.

HENRIETTE.

DAY or two after the Sunday on which Dick Lindsay was thus affected, Lady Margery, being "on duty," passed along the corridor which led to the apartments of the Duchess of York, and knocked at the door of the tiring room. When she entered she found Mary Beatrice in demi-toilette, her beautiful hair released from its stiff plaits and flowing over her shoulders. Near her was seated a lady to whom Margery had never spoken, but whom she had often seen in the chapel, not unfrequently shedding tears as she listened to Père de la Colombière's sermons. She was about eight-and-twenty, and of rare beauty, while her dress, of the richest materials and the height of fashion, showed she was a person of rank and wealth.

"O, it is you, my May-blossom!" said the Duchess. "You see I have not yet begun to dress. I sent away Elise and Fanchette, and

told them to come back in half an hour, for
I wanted to have a chat with the Duchesse
de Marigny. No, you need not run away,
ma petite," continued the Princess, as Margery retreated towards the door, "our secrets
are all said; and if *you* do overhear me eulo-
gizing our good chaplain, and begging Henriette not to give up coming to hear him,
you won't betray me. She says she will
never come again—she fears lest his words
should take too great a hold on her. What
say you, *miladi* May? Let us hear one of
those rare sayings of yours which are so
wise."

May smiled gaily at what she took to be a
jest, and then, looking up into the face of the
fashionable lady, for whom she had so often
secretly prayed, and who, in her turn was
gazing with some curiosity at the young girl,
she said:

"Would it not, your Highness, be a good
thing if Madame la Duchesse saw our reverend Father himself?"

Mary Beatrice laughed outright.

"Well done, May; you have said that at
once which I have been lacking courage to
propose."

"O do, Madame," continued May, blushing to her temples with timidity, yet firmly
persevering in her purpose. " The Father
is so good and gentle, he will listen to your
difficulties with patience."

There was an expression of irresolution on
the face of the Duchesse de Marigny, and she
answered not.

"Yes, Henriette," said Mary Beatrice, "she
says well; go into my small withdrawing-
room, and I will send for him, and you can
entertain him till I am dressed."

May obeyed a sign, and went instantly to
summon Père de la Colombière, and, in a few
minutes, the Duchesse de Marigny found
herself in his presence."

"I am sorry, Father," she began, "that her
Highness should have troubled you to come
to me. A saint herself, this young and noble
Princess, she wants all she cares for to be so
also. But," added she, with a smile, "I have
no fancy for that."

"And yet," said the Father, "report has
told, me Madame, that you are diligent in
taking the first steps to sanctity."

"I hardly know what you mean, Father

unless it be that I have some respect for my
name, that I do not stoop to degrading vices,
and that I hear Mass every Sunday in the
Queen's chapel at Whitehall."

"That *is* what I mean," returned he;
"and in these days it is much; and our good
and dear Lord, who is so grievously offended
in this city, is consoled by your fidelity, and
will reward it. He will draw you onwards
by His grace to find the delights of His
service."

Madame de Marigny sighed.

"What is your great difficulty, Madame?"
pursued the Father. "You are Catholic
by birth. What is it that prevents you from
giving yourself to God? If I mistake not,
your position renders you peculiarly free."

"In one sense, yes, Father. Since my
husband's death I am my own mistress. No
one can dictate to me how I should dispose
of my fortune or regulate my time; but,
Father, there are the ties of long habit. I
was not brought up piously. My family,
though never actually giving up the Faith,
"conformed to the times" as much as they
could. Comfort and ease and luxury have

been mine since my childhood. My mar
riage was a happy one; my husband, indul-
gence itself. He was, as you know, a Frenchman, and troubled himself little about
religion."

"Well, so much for the past," said the
Father, as she paused. "But, for the future,
God is speaking to your heart. Your friendship for the Duchess of York, and the kindness you have shown her, of which she has
told me, assure me that good inspirations
are flowing into your soul."

"Religion frightens me, mon Père," said
Madame de Marigny. "I see the Duchess
living the life almost of a saint. I looked
at that little favorite of hers who came to
call you to me, and I see the face of an angel.
I know what Lord Stafford's daughters are,
and a number of others. I have no taste for
piety. I like the world and its enjoyments.
I cannot be bound to control my actions and
watch over my thoughts. I must be free."

"It is true," answered the Father, "that
the Princess whom I serve is one of rare
piety. It is true that there are some souls I
know of in London who are called to great

perfection, and who are following that call. But God's ways are not the same for all. 'One star differeth from another star in glory.' God calls us all to save our souls, and to keep His commandments. This is all we, His unworthy ministers, have a right to ask in His name. As to what farther He will do with the soul that obeys His law is His own work. Impelled by the whisperings of His grace, many a one who gave Him but little to begin with has given Him all without a struggle. There are souls who press onwards in the road to heaven; and we even who are vowed to His service—we, the guides of the flock—can only look up in secret wonder, as we see them far on before us. But," added he, turning to Henriette, with that winning smile that often broke like sunlight over his face, "perhaps you, Madame, are only destined to remain in the ranks of the army, and not to be put in a post of danger."

The lady laughed, but not joyously. Then the Father continued in his grave tones·

"But, Madame, are you really in those

ranks? Are you, indeed, on Christ's side in the combat?"

Madame de Marigny covered her face with her hands.

"I have not been to confession for two years," she replied. "Until the Duchess of York came here I did not care about it, but the sight of her sweet face has often given me remorse. I saw her amidst all her temptations and trials leading a holy life. Since you have been here I have heard almost every sermon you have given. Often have your words pierced my heart; but the one you preached last Sunday on confession seemed made for me. When you said, 'Throw your eyes over your past life, scarcely can you find a year, a day, an hour of innocence,' you were describing me. When you declared that God said, 'Return, however; come back from thy wanderings, I am ready to receive thee. Is it not time to come at last to Me? Knowest thou not I am thy Father? Why wilt thou forget Me, although thou dost receive each day from My hand thy life, and all the good things of life?' the call seemed addressed to me. And when, finally,

you said, 'Go without fear—Go and plunge
into the Blood of Jesus Christ—go and
regain in that sacred flood a beauty that
shall delight the angels, and gain for you
the Heart of God Himself;' at that moment
I longed to throw myself at your feet, Father,
and implore you to reconcile me with God.
But, the sermon ended, I had to return to
Whitehall. The world regained its power;
I cannot give it up, Father—it is so sweet;
and this is why I said to the Duchess I would
not come again, and begged her to fill up
my place."

"And will you really, Madame, go on risk-
ing your soul's salvation? For you know
that, should death overtake you, your fate
would be terrible."

"No, Father; I will come to confession.
Lent is at hand, and I will not let another
Easter pass over my head without the Sacraments. Father, if you will have patience to
interest yourself with such a being, I would
implore you to hear me; but I wish not to
deceive you. I cannot join this band of
devoted souls you are leading to perfection.
cannot give up the world—it is too sweet."

"I will be content with what you offer me," said the Father, smiling again, but a little sadly this time, "and I promise you that prayers shall rise up to Heaven for you. I possess in France, and here also, a treasure worth far more to me than gold or gems—the prayers of holy souls which are willingly given when I ask for them. They are prayers that can 'pierce the clouds.' They shall be offered for you. Farewell!" —and, as she knelt weeping at his feet, he blessed her and withdrew. He returned to his room, and, after spending a short time in prayer before the Blessed Sacrament, resumed his seat at his writing-table.

Père de la Colombière spent much time in correspondence, and thus kept up intercourse with several convents, and many individuals who had been under his direction in France. Indeed, from his letters, we gather that many were directed by him still by means of correspondence.

A week or two after the interview we have recorded, during which time he had seen Henriette de Marigny more than once, he wrote as follows to a Superior of a

Convent, probably one of the Visitation Order:

"LONDON.

"I write to you, Reverend Mother, to tell you how grieved I am at what is passing around you. Letters reached me yesterday which gave me great pain, and, if I did not feel a firm hope in the mercy of God that He will take care of His good children, I could hardly be consoled. What misery it would be if, while our Lord is blessing our labors here, the enemy of our salvation should destroy elsewhere that which I had the consolation to establish with His mercy. I thank our Lord for having given me consolation by your pious letters, and I hope to derive profit from them. I really need this help, for here, Reverend Mother—I cannot tell you so too plainly—the dangers are infinite, and one has no other help than that which comes from God.

"I have many good works on hand, all concerning the sanctification or conversion of souls. I feel an increasing zeal to aid those who wish to tend after perfection, and to give the desire for it to those who have it not.

"There is at court a young widow about twenty-seven or twenty-eight years of age, who, amidst the almost universal corruption, has an unstained reputation, although her beauty and wit expose her to great dangers. This lady, who is of the highest rank, never misses any of my sermons, and often sheds tears at them before everybody. She has often desires of giving herself to God, and even of giving up all things; but she is rich, she is in the *éclat* of the world, she cannot resolve to renounce vanity. Her natural dispositions are good. I have spoken to her strongly. She listens with pleasure; but I do not see that I make any progress. She admires what is good, but has not the strength of will to embrace it. I have a great repugnance in going to see her, but I continue to go, for I have felt the same in the case of persons who finally were led back to God, and I do not desire to know what our Lord asks from me; I am contented to work on in uncertainty, only I fear to lose time which I could better employ elsewhere.

"If this lady were to do much for God, it would be a great example, for assuredly there is no other woman at Court who can be compared to her as regards her qualities of body and soul. Pray to our good God about this. I never forget you, but I will try to remember your community more especially during your retreat. I hope God will give me grace to begin one the day after to-morrow, of which I stand in great need. I am entirely yours in our Lord.　　　　　LA COLOMBIERE."

CHAPTER X.

DICK LINDSAY.

MOONSTRUCK, Dick?" said Philip Engelby to his friend, as they met in Birdcage Walk on a night when the summer moon shed a flood of silvery light over the Park, while the palace of St. James' lay deep in shadow.

Dick was slowly passing up and down, his eyes fixed on that same shadowy pile.

Philip drew Dick's arm within his own.

"Poor fellow," he said, "so the pang has come to you at last! I thought you would get off scot free, you seemed to take life so easily, and now it seemeth unto me the disease is worse with you than with many of us."

"I would rather have known it and suffered," said Dick, in a grave tone, that Philip hardly ever remembered hearing him use, "than to have gone on as I was, a mere dangler and court-fool. It hath made a man of me; and, all unworthy as I am, perchance my

faithful devotion may win a reward at last.
For this I wait, and long and hope. I can
be as patient as Job if need be. Tell me,
Phil," asked he eagerly, "dost think there
is *any* hope for me?"

"My dear fellow," responded Philip, with
real kindness, "I should say not; but woman
is such a perfect enigma one can never tell.
If I have read Margery aright, none but a
Papist will ever win her favor. She is a
dévote—a fanatic."

Dick pulled away his arm abruptly.

"She is an angel!" he cried; "I was baptized a Catholic, as well you know. I remember me yet of the *Ave Maria* I muttered
at my mother's knee. Of late I have lived
without religion; for all this turmoil and din
of tongues, men calling on God to sanction
their own hates, and enable them to work
out their own ambition, is abhorrent to me.
These persecutions—these changes of faith,
that a man may wear a crown, or get a fat
place about court, are not akin to that faith my
mother preached to me. If Margery should
be mine, I would say to her, as Ruth to
Naomi, 'Thy people shall be my people, and
thy God my God.'"

" You mean you'll turn Papist?" said Phil, in astonishment.

" Even so."

" Dick, you are mad, verily distraught. Some one ought to tend you in your sickness. Turn Papist, man, for the sake of a girl!" and then Philip laughed bitterly.

Dick turned away, and began to walk in the opposite direction; but Philip pursued him, and put his hand on his shoulder. The other impatiently shook him off.

" Pshaw! Dick, don't be a fool. Haven't I been through it all myself?"

" No!" cried Dick, indignantly, turning upon him; " you never knew what it was to love, or you could not jest and sneer and doubt as you do now."

Philip's tone suddenly changed. He again drew his friend's arm within his own.

"I am to blame, Dick; I crave pardon. Believe me, 'tis my own suffering that makes me bitter. Now, tell me, can I do aught for you with this lady of your thoughts?"

"Yes," said Dick, eagerly; "give me speech of her without eavesdroppers. I can never see her save when a dozen eyes are watching us. Methinks she knows—she must know —the secret of my devotion; but never have I had an opportunity of whispering it to her."

"I'll manage it," cried Phil. "Come to the Palace to-morrow night, or, rather, to-night. I believe it hath long since chimed midnight. If the weather holds, as it surely will, the Duchess goeth into the gardens, the company break up into groups, and it will go hard if I cannot manage to gain speech for you with her. And now let us go to our lodgings," and so saying, he led Dick through a gate standing nearly in the same position as the one now admitting from Birdcage Walk to St. James' street. They then paused before the porch of the Palace. "Seest thou that light, Dick," said Phil, pointing to a dim twinkle in a small window on the third floor. "There is the Jesuit plotter keeping his vigil. Mayhap what mischief he broweth now."

"I don't believe a word of it!" said Dick, stoutly. "The man is as good and honest a one as I ever saw. He practices what he preaches, which is a good deal more than the parsons and bishops do, who wink at royal crimes and hang on to the great. This man cringes to no one, curries favor with none. And if these priests are what I have been taught to believe, how is it that women like unto my fair lady, to the Howard damsels, the Duchess herself, and a host more, are the result of their teaching? I am told these creatures are ruled by priests, brought up by them, and under their control, and I find, as the fruits of it, the modesty and purity that one might otherwise believe to have fled from earth. I find the true wife and the obedient child. I see them kind to the suffering, and forgetful of self; and I turn to our Protestant women—faugh! it sickens me. Here we are, I see. Good night, Phil," and Dick dashed up the street in which he lodged.

Philip looked after him.

"They'll not have much trouble with him, poor fellow. 'Twixt love and controversy poor Dick's head will not keep steady on his shoulders. Well, there's no help for it; if he will run his head against a wall, he must, and there's an end on't."

CHAPTER XI.

A BEACON STAR.

THE day, as Philip had foretold, proved fine, and the company who assembled in the Palace wandered into the gardens. Philip hastened to the side of Marguerite. She was looking *distraite*, for her idol, Lady Diana, was absent, and Philip was welcomed with a smile. She was beginning to look in the face the prospect of marrying him. He was rapidly rising in favor with Lord Edenhall, and the idea of uniting the wealth and title of her family was a pleasing one to Marguerite.

She was certain she should never love anyone as she loved her idolized friend, and she looked on marriage as a necessity of life which she must adopt. Poor Marguerite! religion was losing its hold on her; the pride and self-will of her character, which had given so much anxiety to the nuns of the Visitation, developed themselves.

The idea of renouncing her religion was

abhorrent to her. She could not make herself disbelieve—faith burned too brightly in her soul; for often, how often that light burns on when the oil of charity has wasted away, and the thick smoke of worldliness has done its best to smother the flame. Marguerite believed; occasionally she went to confession; she had a great reverence for Père de la Colombière, but as yet even his voice could not persuade her to moderate her attachment for Lady Diana or approach Holy Communion. On this point she was obdurate, and thus her soul, deprived of all inward peace, sought eagerly after sympathy and distraction.

Philip was welcomed, as we have said, and he presently began, with an amused smile,

"Fairest coz, I would engage you in a state plot."

"And endanger my neck," said Marguerite, laughing.

"Not so, for the court I speak of is the court of love, and there the only penalties are arrows. I mean, to speak plainly, that I want to give Dick Lindsay a chance of pleading his cause with your sister. I have promised him I would seek an occasion."

"Dick Lindsay!" said Marguerite, scornfully; but as the remembrance he was Lady Diana's brother flashed on her mind, the lines of her face softened. "Nay, Philip, this is folly," she continued, "you know May will not listen to him."

"But he wants to plead his own cause; 'tis hard to linger on unheard. A man will not believe that his own eloquence can be resisted. See, there he is, sauntering about most disconsolate. Poor Dick! verily he weareth his heart on his sleeve. Be merciful, Marguerite."

"Go and look for May," said his cousin, with a smile. "Tell her she will find me in the summer-house by the fountain. Then you and Dick must enter while I am conferring with her, and some way or other *we* must contrive to get out of the way."

Philip obeyed his orders, and found May and Alethea Howard side by side not far from the Duchess. May instantly rose at her sister's summons, and hastened to the summer-house.

"See, darling," said Marguerite, as she entered, "how I have torn this lace. I am ashamed to go about in such a fashion. Can't you manage with your deft fingers to settle it for me?"

May immediately set about the task, and the trifling injury was almost repaired when Philip and Dick entered.

"Oh, May," cried Marguerite, springing up, "wait here one moment for me. I want particularly to present you to Lady Travers; 'tis my father's wish we treat her with respect, and I see her passing even now; tarry one instant, and you shall fasten on the rest of the lace for me. Philip Engelby, your escort, sir. I commend my sister to your good offices, Master Lindsay," and, in an instant, the two were gone, leaving May bewildered, blushing and embarrassed.

Desperation gave Dick courage. Time was precious, and this was his only chance.

"Lady Margery," he faltered, "pardon me, this is my doing—'tis a *ruse* practised on you out of compassion for me. Fairest lady, you must surely have seen the state of my heart. I know my own unworthiness, but I crave some hope from you—my life's-blood should be shed willingly if you need it."

Although she trembled and flushed pain-fully, May was calm and dignified.

"I thank you, sir, for the honor you proffer me," she said, with gentleness; "but I pray you dismiss the thought—it is impossible!"

"Oh, pardon me," said Dick, and a look of veritable anguish was on his face. "Pardon the question—doth another possess this heart, or can time, patience, all you will, win you? I am not of your faith, I know; but I intend so to become, if you bid me. If indeed that heart of yours be free, let me, at least, try by faithful devotion to win it."

May hesitated for a moment, then she spoke with firmness:

"My heart is *not* free—it is bestowed, and that for aye."

Dick bowed his head like a man who receives sentence of death, and he said, in a changed voice:

"I will not detain you, Lady Margery; let me lead you to your sister."

May took a great and sudden resolution.

"Master Lindsay, you spoke erewhile of faith; deem you so lightly of it that you would change a real conviction for the sake of a woman's smile?"

"No," he answered, "but your faith wins monstrously on one who, like myself, hath been tossed on a weary sea of doubt and contempt. I have had no more religion than a dog—I can see none in the prattling of these parsons, or the fulminations of my lord of London. Willingly would I have followed you as a little child, to learn the faith that shines in your eyes and in those of your royal mistress."

May raised those sweet dove-like eyes, and, for the first time, fixed them on Dick.

"Richard Lindsay," she said, "I will be true with you, I will trust you. My heart is given to God; I can love none but Him. If it be His will, I would fain be hidden in a cloister, but even if not, I have no place for an earthly affection."

As she spoke these words, she looked so spiritualized, so rapt from the things of earth, that Dick gazed at her in astonished reverence. He muttered to himself, when she had finished, "A cloister, a living tomb."

"No," said May, firmly, "believe it not. Look at the world around you—see how fairly it shines on me, yet it hath no charms. A voice sweeter than those of earth calleth me away. A joy which none can know save to whom it is given allures my heart. Then will you not believe there is some mystery in this—will you not credit that th s faith which draws me from all you hold dear has a depth you have never seen? Promise me to seek it, promise me to search into it, to seek for yourself if my words be truth."

"I will promise," said Dick, looking at her with adoration. "Think not too harshly of me if I say I cling to the link that will thus bind me to you. I will follow you as my beacon star."

A wan smile broke over his face.

"I must fasten your glove in my helmet as the Knights of the Table Round, and go forth on my quest of the San Greal."

May clasped her hands.

"Ah, in very truth!" she said, "set forth on that quest, and the quaint old story shall turn into reality. You shall find the San Greal; and, when the seeker found it, says the legend, he was fully repaid, and the beacon star melted away into the light of day."

As she spoke these last words, she glided by him, and vanished into the crowd.

Dick soon after made his escape from the gardens, and, from that day forth, the whole tenor of his life was changed.

CHAPTER XII.

LADY DI'S PROJECT.

T last Lady Diana was released from the task she had found so irksome. Sir David Villiers died, and Lady Diana was free. For the first few days she was full of rejoicing. She had no fear of losing her position at court, for it had been the King's appointment, against which neither James nor Mary Beatrice would venture to rebel. Besides, with consummate tact, she had contrived to make herself liked by both Duke and Duchess. Over Mary Beatrice she even exercised a sort of baneful influence, for the Princess was extremely young, naturally clinging and diffident, and terribly afraid of compromising her husband by any ill-judged act on her part.

Never, perhaps, was Princess placed in a more cruel position than Mary Beatrice. In pleasing the King, she generally contrived to displease the Queen, and then often found the fault of not keeping in the good graces of both was laid on her.   Lady Diana, with her winning manners, her knowledge of court secrets, her fearless bearing towards the King, and her intimacy with the Queen, possessed great power over Mary Beatrice.

Lady Diana's delight at her widowdhood was of short duration.   Sir David Villiers' estates were entailed, and passed to a distant relative; and the riches which his wife believed him to have accumulated, and which were to pass to her, were found not to exist. He had always been obstinately silent with his wife as to the disposition of his moneys, and now she found they had melted away. So, save for her place at court, Lady Diana found herself as poor as when she broke her plight with Philip.

The disappointment was bitter.   It is difficult to estimate the effect of such on her character.   She had hardened her conscience, had deadened her better instincts to obtain wealth and power, and now they were snatched from her.   Riches in her eyes were of a value past all words to describe.   How was she to satisfy her inordinate love of dress?

How was she to be, as heretofore, the best-dressed woman at court, the person who led the fashion, whose attire had always been a marvel of elegant taste and costliness? The family jewels passed away from her. How was she to replace them? How was she to gratify her chief amusement (which with her was a passion), card-playing? All these thoughts ran through her brain as she sat alone in her chamber, and her resolution was taken. Ere she laid aside her widow's mourning she would win a greater prize, she would attain a higher position. Her present one was dependent on court favor, and this should no longer be. Lady Diana smoothed her brow, arranged her widow's coif in the most becoming manner she could, and went forth from her chamber.

"Dearest Rita," said she, when she next met her devoted satelite, revolving as ever round her planet, "you must be all to me now. I am alone in the world. Even poor Dick is not to be counted on. He is out of his senses, I suppose, for he hath forsworn the world altogether. I warrant he will seek foreign parts and become a monk. Poor Dick!"

And Lady Di laughed merrily at the idea of gay, dashing Dick hiding himself under a monk's cowl, and passing from a dangler of fashion to a tiller of the ground.

"Dearest and lovely friend," said Rita, kissing her hand in a transport of delight, "if I can only be a comfort to you, my whole life will be well spent."

"Pshaw, child!" retorted Lady Di, "have you not to marry?"

"O, not at present!" cried Rita, "and perhaps never. Or, if," she added, "it must be, I am sure—" she stopped, blushing.

She did not actually like to speak of Philip as her future husband, though the thought in her mind was that Philip would not interfere with her devotion to her friend. Marguerite was ignorant of the passages between Philip and Di Lindsay. May, believing her to know it, had never mentioned what she had heard, and, as often happens in life, the person supposed by everyone to know a fact was the only one in ignorance. No one ventured to talk of Lady Diana in Marguerite's presence; therefore she remained uninformed on the matter.

But she had seen signs of devotion to Lady
Diana in Philip, which she had interpreted
in her own way; and, besides, she felt very
sure that though Philip sought her hand, he
did not care to win her heart, nor to bestow
his on her.   It was this conviction that made
Marguerite look quiety forward to a union
with him, knowing that she should accept
him without affection, and simply to carry
out her object of placing herself in her right
position.   She felt she would do him no
injustice.

Lady Diana smiled.

"I will finish your sentence for you, *chère*,
'Philip would not interfere.'   But, Rita, it is
not settled you are to wed Philip, and I, for
one, see no reason why you should."

Marguerite opened her eyes wide.

"I thought," she faltered, "you wished it,
you advised it.   'Tis because of what you
said that I have suffered him to pay me court
of late."

"Never mind that, Rita.   I have pondered
over the subject, and I think it would not be
a prudent match for you.   It is true your
dower is large, but that is no reason you are
to marry a poor man."

"But I thought—you know we planned," said Marguerite, still bewildered with the sudden change, "that to unite the title and lands together would be a good thing."

"That is the very point," returned Lady Diana. "I have considered it—it looked feasible at first. But what, Rita, should hinder your father from wedding again?"

As she spoke, she fixed her eyes keenly on Marguerite's face; she beheld it flush crimson, and tears of indignation sprang to Rita's eyes.

An idolizing friendship deadens, but does not destroy, the traditions of one's life.

"Never!" cried the girl, breathlessly. "He never forgets my mother. He would never put any one in her place; he said so when she died, for Louise told us so, and he never changes his word."

Lady Di's lip curled.

"My dear Rita, I thought you were no longer a child, like May. As if a man really cherished a romance like this. He may think he does; but, if either love or policy told him to wed again, trust me he would do so."

"I am sure he would not," said Rita, indignantly, her eyes flashing. "You do not know him, Lady Di; you do not know the Edenhall nature;" and Rita arched her neck and drew herself up to her full height, like a young war-horse ready for battle.

Never. had Lady Diana seen such an exhibition of passion in the girl's nature. She stood aloof as if she had been stung. There was no trace of the yielding docility, the adoring submission, Lady Di was accustomed to receive. She saw that it was quite possible Rita would break loose from her allegiance, and prove a very rebel. Quick as lightning Lady Diana's plans were formed.

"True enough, darling, I do not know an Edenhall's nature; but, without knowing, I have learned to love it," and she extended her hand towards Marguerite. "You know your father, and your word is enough—I'll put aside for the future such a thought as treason. Pardon me, dearest. You know I am a worn-out woman and you a fresh maiden, who has not had her belief in truth and honor rudely shattered to pieces;" and, as she said these words in a low, mournful tone, she covered her face with her hands, as if overcome with emotion.

In an instant Rita was kneeling by her side, imploring forgiveness for having grieved her. It was sweetly given; but Lady Diana did not recover her spirits in Rita's presence, and the poor girl went away sad at heart.

As soon as she was alone, Lady Diana's face changed.

"Well-a-day," she said to herself, "I must give up that idea. What does a girl's love matter to me? If she be fool enough to wed Phil, let her do it—she'll reck the day; but my plans are not to be marred by her folly. I will brush her out of my path, if need be, as I would an insect."

Thus thought Lady Di, while Marguerite lay weeping on her bed, pondering how she could best comfort her heart's idol.

CHAPTER XIII.

THE MAYFAIR FARM.

FROM that time forward Lady Diana spared no pains to captivate Marguerite, and she accepted the invitations lavished on her of visiting Lord Edenhall's house in Pall Mall. Up to this time the acquaintance of the Earl and his daughter's friend had been slight and distant, and it was some little time before the stern and self-contained man yielded to the fascination of the clever woman who had made up her mind she would charm him. But she succeeded at length, and Lord Edenhall was never so pleased as when Lady Diana was his daughter's guest. Marguerite had never known before how brilliant and sparkling her father could be till Lady Diana drew him out. Never had she been so happy. Religion was nearly thrown overboard in her dream of delight. She still attended Mass in the Royal Chapel, and tried to shut the ears of her mind to Père de la

Colombière's discourses. She avoided meeting him, and totally neglected the Sacraments. She was wrapped up and absorbed in a dream of earthly love, and the merciful Father, who never punishes save in compassion, and never corrects save to heal, was watching the time when the dream should be dispelled, and a rude awakening take place.

The only member of the Edenhall family with whom Lady Diana did not succeed was May. She could cast no glamor over that fair young mind. The clouds flit over the clear waters of a lake, but they do not stir its depths. So was it with the soul of Margery; and Lady Diana, finding her arts fail, did her best to keep out of Margery's way. The poor child had never had such liberty before. She found Marguerite planning for her how she should spend some days at Kensington, or how she should meet Alethea, till her heart bounded again with joy at this new considerateness on the part of a sister who had been latterly so forgetful of her.

It thus came to pass that May and Alethea were both present at a conference given by

Père de la Colombière to the Nuns of the Conception living at the grange or farm to which we once led our readers. It was the Feast of the Visitation, and a day to be marked forever in the lives of the two young maidens. We will tell the reason of their joy in Father de la Colombière's own words. On this day he wrote as follows to a Visitation nun in France:

"We are keeping the Feast of the Visitation, and have, thanks be to God, celebrated it well, considering the country we are in; besides many persons who went to communion, there were two young ladies about twenty years of age who chose this day to consecrate themselves to God by a vow of perpetual chastity, after having made a general confession. Upon one of these girls God is beginning to pour very special graces.

"Our Lord sends me every day souls which seem to me to be chosen ones, and who give themselves to Him most generously. Three are now thinking of entering religion, and two others have been under my care for some time who are not far off from it. I have sent off the two men who wished to enter religion, and of whom I wrote to you. Ask our Lord to give them real inspirations. I write to you this good news of what I believe God is preparing for His glory. As for me, I do nothing. I am not eager, and I remark that our Lord sends me, after waiting three, four and five months, souls whom I would scarcely have dared to ask for. Please give us your prayers, for, if you will thus help me, I hope our Lord will not regard my sins, and will be greatly glorified in this city. Ever yours in Jesus Christ, LA COLOMBIERE."

Very radiant were the faces of May and Alethea as they took their places among the nuns to listen to the long-promised description of the holy nun of Paray-le-Monial.

"I need hardly remind you, my Sisters," said the Father, "of those words of Holy Writ, 'Wonderful is God in His saints.' You have pondered over them often, and you have tried to comprehend this great lesson that God chooses to work in His poor creatures, 'Greater things than these ye shall do, because I go to the Father.' He is knit up with us, for do we not feed upon His Body and Blood? Therefore, wondrous are the works He shall do in a soul that corresponds to His grace, that gives herself up to His love. There are many such souls on earth now, Sisters, and I believe it has been my singular privilege to be brought into

communication with one of them. About
two years ago, I was sent to be Superior of
our residence at Paray-le-Monial, a small in-
significant town in Burgundy. There exists
there a Convent of the Visitation Order,
founded by Father de Barry, of our company. The holy founders of the Order were
both living at the time, and, with their blessing, the little colony came forth from Lyons.
More than once the saintly Madame de
Chantal (who will, I feel sure, be ere long
raised upon the altars of the church) visited
this house, and thus left a benediction rest-
ing on it.

"As I told you on a former occasion, the
Superior of the Visitation placed Sister Margaret Mary Alacoque under my direction,
and thus I became acquainted with the mar-
vels of grace passing in this soul.

"Our Blessed Lord has appeared to her
frequently, and may be said to guide her by
the words of His own lips. Only as He who
was subject for thirty years to his own creatures, would ever impress on his children
that the path he loves for them is that of
obedience, He would not permit this holy

soul to obey even His own words, without referring to her director, however unworthy that latter might be. One day, she said to our dear Lord: 'But to whom, Lord, dost Thou address Thyself? To a poor creature and to so wretched a sinner that her unworthiness would be capable of hindering the accomplishment of Thy design. Thou hast so many generous souls to execute it.' And our merciful Lord, who loves also that His children be like unto Himself, meek and lowly, deigned thus to answer: 'What! do you not know that I make use of the weakest instruments to confound the strong? that it is in the little and poor of spirit that My power commonly manifests itself with the greatest splendor, in order that they may attribute nothing to themselves?' And then she, simple and fearless as a child with its mother, made answer to her dearest Master: 'Do Thou, then, give me the means of doing what Thou commandest.' He answered: 'Address yourself to My servant, Claude de la Colombière, and tell him from Me to do what he can to establish this devotion, and to give this pleasure to My Divine Heart.

Let him not be discouraged at the difficulties
he will meet with, for there will be no lack
of them; but he must remember that those
are all-powerful who distrust themselves and
place their whole confidence in me.' "

Here Father de la Colombière paused, and
seemed to wish the sisters themselves to
speak.

Mother Elizabeth remarked:

"Father, is this saint as yet hidden in her
community, or do all around her appreciate
her great gifts and graces?"

"Thanks be to God," answered the Father,
"as yet she is hidden, and has to suffer, as
far as it is possible to suffer in a holy and
fervent community. The Visitation nuns
are trained to have a horror of singularity;
it is a tradition of their Order, and they do
well to be jealous of it. Therefore, Sister
Margaret has naturally something to undergo, and she rejoices in it. Her virtue,
my Sisters, is solid; profoundly humble,
humiliation and reproach are her delight.
She was thoroughly tried in her novitiate.
Often was she sent to make her meditation
while sweeping the court, but no outward

employment could distract her from union with our Lord.

"And now, Sisters, let us learn a lesson from this holy soul. I want to instil in you all a great love and devotion to the Sacred Heart of Jesus. That heart was cleft open for us on Calvary, let us hide ourselves within it. That heart broke with love for us, let us at least give our hearts in return if we cannot make them break with love for Him. I want you to cultivate in yourselves a special devotion to the adorable humanity of our Divine Lord.

"From this revelation to Sister Margaret Alacoque, it is certain such a devotion must be most acceptable to Him. I shall come hither again, Sisters, if Father Whitbread sends me, for I desire, if our Lord permit me, to kindle in the hearts of all religious an intense devotion to the Heart of Jesus. I believe that God has destined this to be an especial work of the Company, and, for some mysterious reason, He has chosen the most unworthy of its sons to sow the first seed—others shall water, He shall give the increase. Who knoweth," said the Father, while a flush came into his usually pale face, and his eyes lit up with a celestial light, "whether, on this very spot, a shrine may not arise wherein that Sacred Heart shall be specially honored and invoked?

"Oh, Sisters, let us take courage: the sky is black overhead, and heavy with clouds; imprisonment, torture and death may be your portion, but God's works shall never perish. Sooner or later, the faith shall arise again in England. Sooner or later, the Virgin Mother, whose feast we keep to-day, shall again reign over the land that once was hers from North to South, from East to West. England is the first country in which the voice of a Catholic priest has dared to proclaim the devotion to the Sacred Heart. Believe my words, Sisters, I speak the truth, by the devotion to the Sacred Heart, England shall be saved.

"Oh, to win this fair gem for our Master's royal crown, shall we not give our prayers, our sufferings, our lives, our all?"

Unable to restrain his emotion, Father de la Colombière quitted the room.

CHAPTER XIV.

THE BEGINNING OF THE SNARE.

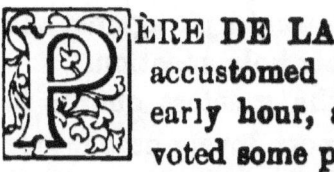ÈRE DE LA COLOMBIÉRE was accustomed to say Mass at a very early hour, and he generally devoted some part of the morning to his correspondence and study. Those who wished for his counsel knew they might freely interrupt him at any time. Indeed he rarely went out, and when he did so it was simply to go to the assistance of some one who could not or would not come to him.

As for court life, it flowed by the Father as a brawling stream may flow at a mountain's foot, and not disturb a blade of grass on the surface; in its turmoil he took no part. The pleasures for which people were daily perilling their souls, the amusements which to many were an engrossing snare, were absolutely harmless to one who had long since "bartered earth for heaven." Had duty obliged him to mingle in court circles, he would have obeyed, but while his body was there his soul would have been far away. But this was not required of him; young as Mary Beatrice was, she had sense to discern some of the eminent gifts of her chaplain. She scrupulously avoided asking him to do aught which would jar against the habits of his life and his holy vocation.

Unselfishness was the greatest charm in the character of this most lovely among our princesses. She loved to see others avail themselves of his ministry, and, as we have seen in the case of the Duchesse de Marigny, did not hesitate in certain cases to advise it. Therefore Père de la Colombière could truly say, as he did in his letters, he could keep his rule as well in the Palace as in a college of the society.

One morning, when he was saying his Office, a knock came to the door; on opening it he found a young man of pleasing appearance, but shabbily dressed, who asked to speak to him.

The Father received him cordially, and invited him to be seated.

"You are French, I think," added he, glancing at his visitor.

"Yes, Father, I am from Dauphiné; my name is Arsène Le Noir; I have come to tell you my history," and he cast his eyes on the ground. "My family were extremely poor, but a charitable lady, Madame Chatelaine, of our village, took a fancy to me—or compassion on me, perhaps it would be more true to say—and taught me many things. Then, thinking I was too good—I mean, mon Père, unfitted for the life of a peasant—she persuaded her eldest son to take me with him to Paris as a page; but, alas, in Paris my master was killed in a duel, having lost largely at play the preceeding night, and all his suite were abruptly dismissed. Starvation stared me in the face, when an English milord, who had seen me at my master's house, and now happened to meet me wandering about the streets, had compassion on me, took me into his service, and brought me to England. In his household I have grown up. Treated with scant kindness by my master and with cruelty by his menials, I have been unable to practice my religion, though I cling to it in my heart."

"Have you, my son," said the Father, "in any way consented to the Protestant belief?"

The young man threw himself on his knees before the priest.

"Father, I have, I acknowledge it with shame; not that my faith wavered. No; I have never forgotten my mother's lessons, nor could I ever exchange the majestic worship of the Catholic Church for the cold, barren creed of the Protestant; but, alas! my motive was to curry favor with my master. I felt I was looked on with distrust as a French Papist, and I thought if I conformed that prejudice against me would be removed."

"And has this been the case?" said the Father, gently.

"Yes, Father, my condition hath been greatly bettered. My mistress, who cometh of a Roundhead family, looks with special favor on me. She trusts me more than one of the lackeys who have ever been Protestants."

But here he paused and hid his face in his hands.

Père de la Colombière laid his hand gently on the bowed head.

"Conscience was not still, my son," he said, in a tone of tenderness.

"O, Father," cried Arsène, in a tone of anguish, "methinks I read or heard in my childhood a tale of some man who had a fox secretly gnawing him under his rich apparel and in the midst of every splendor; so it hath been with me; a fox's tooth, in truth, is remorse. By night, by day, I have no rest. I have heard of you for months past, and could not summon strength to come and throw myself at your feet. Oftentimes have I lingered in the street, looking up to the solitary light which I guessed was burning in your chamber, for I knew, Father, you would pray when all the world were asleep. At those hours willingly would I have burst in upon you, but then the Palace doors were shut, and when the daylight came my courage melted away. At last I could wait no longer, I know not why; perchance some holy soul hath prayed specially for a sinner. Some invisible power hath pushed me to grace; but, Father, is there mercy for me?"

"My son, you know well there is mercy for all; your own heart tells you this. If a human being can listen to your tale only w.th compassion or with love, how much

more must not that Good Shepherd yearn
over you who, for your sake, was content to
lay down His life? Fear not; soon you
shall be safe in the fold; even now He is
drawing you from the thorns and briars, and
carrying you on His shoulders. But first, I
would speak of your temporal affairs," and
Arsène again seated himself. "I suppose
there is no possibility of your remaining in
your present service, and of practicing your
religion in secret, therefore, what purpose
you to do? How long a time will it be
before you can discharge yourself from your
duties there?"

"Father, if it were possible, I would never
return. If I take away either garments or
wages I am certain my lord will have me
pursued and cast into prison. All I have I
owe to him; 'tis true I have labored in
return, but you know how little any plea will
avail when 'tis question of a Protestant
master and Popish servant in this country.
I have put on my worst clothes," continued
he, glancing at his coat. "I do not think
they will grudge me these, and I have writ
a note, saying that the longing to see again

my native land is so strong that I purpose
to work my way to the coast, and thence in
a fishing craft to France. This note will
be discovered in an hour's time, for until
that time no one will look for me. I must
either return and secure the note or fly; but
where, my Father, where can such a wretch
as I find refuge? It seems too much to ask
of your charity, but, if you could help me to
a refuge for a few days only, the labor of my
hands would soon earn my bread."

The Father sat still and silent; a vague
suspicion arose in his mind, and he scruti-
nized the young man from head to foot,
but the ingenuous countenance, the pleading eyes and humble attitude disarmed him.
To seek for proof was useless; in those days,
Catholics had either to trust entirely or instantly resist those who came. Père de la
Colombière chose the first. He drew his
writing materials towards him, and wrote a
few rapid lines. They were addressed to
Master John Aylmer, in the Long Acre.

"Do you know this street, Arsène?"
asked he.

"Yes, Father; I know nigh every street in
London."

"Hasten thither; you will have food and lodging, and all you need. I will be there to-morrow to see you. Hasten, my son, to put your soul in order, to regret the past at the feet of our good Master, and all will be forgiven. Leave the future in the hands of God; He will provide. Now hasten to your destination as quietly as may be."

. With deep gratitude Arsène thanked him, craved his blessing on his knees, and withdrew. As he descended the stairs, his face darkened.

"I love not my part," he said; "it will be weary enough; but what is a poor beggar to do? I should have been found out as an accomplice in that robbery, as sure as fate. I must hide *somewhere*, and to make a proposal as if I was a penitent sinner seemed the most likely. If it has succeeded, I shall have to confess to-morrow: no doubt 'tis part of the *role* I must play. Well-a-days, I have sins enow if I choose to tell them; and, if I don't, I can tell somebody's else, and I am sure I know of plenty. *Allons*, let's toss the cards, and see what turns up in life's game."

CHAPTER XV.

HAPPY MOMENTS.

LADY MARGERY sat at her tambour-frame, giving her whole attention to the work before her, while her sister strolled about the room in a restless, aimless way, now arranging some flowers in a vase, then throwing down a blossom and going quickly to the window to watch for some expected object, always apparently disappointed; then taking up a book and laying it down; then walking up and down the apartment with the impatient tread of one who knows not how to wait. At last, the noise of a lumbering coach made her fly to the window with a look of eager expectation.

"It is for you, May," she cried, in an impatient tone; "it is my Lord Stafford's coach, and Alethea and Kate are both in it. Well, I marvel what pleasure you can find in their company."

"I would give it up any day for thine, my

Rita," said May, passing her arm round her sister.

Marguerite shook off the caress.

"There, get you gone, child," said she, with a heavy sigh; "I am past nursing days. What time was it Alethea promised to come for you? . Perchance our clock hasteneth."

"Eleven of the clock," said May, slowly, for Rita reddened as she spoke.

An hour ago she expected Lady Di, but she could never foretell what freak or mood would seize on that variable being. Marguerite knew the lesson, but had not learned to love it, that she was too often treated as a slave, and Lady Di recked little of letting her waste hours for the fulfillment of an appointment which was kept or not, just as the fancy took her. Yet, entangled in the meshes of her idolatry, the poor child chafed and suffered on. One half the devotion she lavished on Lady Di, turned into another channel, would have made her a saint.

May looked sadly at the wistful face as Rita, glad of something to do, returned to the window to watch Lord Stafford's equipage; and, then, breathing that constant prayer that so often went up from her heart for her sister, she descended the stairs, climbed into the coach, and was warmly greeted by her two friends.

The coach rumbled on its way till it stopped at a house in Piccadilly, a large mansion standing in its own grounds. Lackeys came to the door to assist the ladies to alight, and they were ushered into a specious and handsomely-furnished room on the ground floor. They were hardly seated when a door at the further end opened, and the Duchesse de Marigny glided in. She was elegantly dressed, as when we first saw her, but there was to a keen eye a nameless difference, while the lovely face was fairer than ever, for peace dwelt in the depth of the blue eyes, and the smile around the mouth was no longer forced or vain, but a sign of real happiness.

"Welcome! a thousand welcomes, dear ones!" said she; "come into my withdrawing-room, and we shall be more at our ease."

They followed her into a small room opening from the large *salon* where she usually sat, and where her various occupations were grouped around her.

There was a curious mixture of the surroundings of a great lady, and the employments of one who has found out that time was not given only for amusement.

"Now, my dear ones," cried the Duchesse, gaily, "you must each take something to do, that we may not look like a band of conspirators. May, I can trust your fingers at my tambour-frame. Alethea, don't I pray you, spoil this stocking; and to you, giddy Kate, I shall give the patchwork; you can work at one end and I at the other."

"And then we know which will be best done," retorted Kate.

For a few minutes merry talk went on, till each had settled into her place, so that the servants or anyone entering would have supposed the young ladies had come thither only for a day of chat and pleasure. But an eager look of expectation sat on each young face. It was evident some news from the Duchesse was anxiously looked for.

"Well," said she, laying down her needle and glancing around, "you may guess it was with some reason that I summoned you here to-day. Our good Father wished us to confer together, and he thought that you three might visit me here with less danger of espionage than anywhere else. At the Palace eyes are ever open. Kensington hath enough to bear without any more plots," added she, looking at the Ladies Howard, with a smile. "What think you of the bold project of having a Convent of the Visitation in England?"

May clasped her hands in silent joy; tears came into Alethea's eyes. Kate was the first to speak.

"Now, dearest madame," she said, "an it was on such a project as this you needed our company, confess that I was to come as devil's advocate."

"I plead guilty, Kate; only I must lay some share of the blame on our good Father. 'Bid Katherine thither also,' said he; 'she would throw weight into one scale, and Alethea into the other. She will count the cost ere she consents to any danger for Alethea to run.'"

"He saith truly," answered Katherine, laughing. "The good Father reads me well. No sooner is this convent founded

than off go Alethea and May like birds to
their nest, unheeding of the fowler's snare.
I trow they will be more safe in Paris a
thousand times."

"But, darling Kate, it is surely not our
safety only that is in question," cried Alethea. "If that be a hindrance, we will keep
our purpose and fly to France; but then,
what would it be for England to have the
Saintes Maries in her midst? Did not the
blessed Bishop of Geneva pray for this poor
land, and sigh over it? Would he not willingly have shed his blood for it? Surely, if
his daughters come hither, it shall bring his
benediction on us, and surely his unseen
presence will be amongst us then."

"Yes," said the Duchesse, "and that of his
holy daughter, Jane de Chantal; the pattern,
however far off, to such as I," added she,
smiling. "Methinks, Alethea, I love her
more, if it be possible, than her blessed
Father. To my eager nature, that story of
their last meeting is more edifying than
aught I know in the Lives of the Saints;
to me that act of distinct self-renunciation
would have cost more than many disciplines
unto blood than long fast or hair shirts."

"What story, dear madame?" said Kate. "I am not so learned in the lives of holy people as you are. To tell the truth, I leave the read'ng to Alethea, and look after the household; but, sinner though I be, I love to hear of great deeds wrought by those who are far beyond my gaze. I know Alethea told me how Madame de Chantal stepped over the body of her son, when she left all things to follow her vocation. Alethea meant it, I know, as a hint that it would be useless for me to spread lengthwise on the earth, and hinder her ladyship's progress when once the time hath come, and the good Father hath spoken. As if I could take the trouble—"

A laugh went round the circle as the Sisters exchanged a loving glance.

"Well," said the Duchesse, "to my mind this act of Jane de Chantal of which I speak was greater than that straining of the heart-strings of which you heard. For four years she had never met her spiritual Father, he who knew every fibre of her soul, who alone could counsel and sympathize—letters are but a poor substitute for such intercourse; remember also that, for years, she had been accustomed to receive his constant help; and remember also that she had on her shoulders a heavy weight, the government of her Order, advice to give to others. Ah, how I can enter into her longing for help, for those powerful and pressing words by which light and unction and grace were accustomed to flow into her soul! But the time was coming—she was to meet him at Lyons; there she might speak freely, and so she got her notes ready. Methinks I can see her, and can hear her heart beat with joy as she kneels once more at those revered and beloved feet, and then, sitting down beside him, finds he is going to give her time for a long conference.

"'Which shall speak first,' said he, 'you or I?'

"'I, if it please you,' said the dear soul I love so much. 'My heart hath great need of being reviewed by you.'

"'What! do you still think of self?' replied he, sweetly. (Oh, how severe in reality he was with all his sweetness!) 'I thought to find you altogether angelic; let us speak together of our little congregation, which I love so much because it is the work of God.'

"Then, without a word or thought of complaint, that sweet soul put aside her own wants and desires, and obeyed her Father. For four hours did they hold converse together, but not one word of Jane's own spiritual wants was spoken.

"'We will speak of ourselves at Annecy,' said the Bishop.

"And so Jane de Chantal left him, and departed next day for Grenoble, saying to herself, as she went along, 'Though my father and mother forsake me, the Lord taketh me up.'

"She never saw her spiritual Father again.'

"Never again!" cried Katherine; "not at Annecy, as he promised?"

"He never came again to Annecy in life; he died at Lyons a few days after this interview. It was only his lifeless and precious body that was brought to Annecy, and that rested all one night in the Chapel of the Visitation, and then, in silence and solitude, did that obedient and simple daughter kneel

by the corpse and speak of herself to him.
Oh, surely, though the Church hath not yet
spoken, 'tis no harm to say, 'Jane Frances
de Chantal, pray for me.'"

Here the conversation was interrupted.
A lackey entered to tell his mistress there
were visitors in the *salon*, and, with a look
of dismay at her companions, she obeyed the
summons.

CHAPTER XVI.

THE SEA THAT LIES BETWEEN.

HEN the Duchesse returned to her guests, the conversation was continued. "Well, Kate," said she, "while I have been listening to a most interesting discussion on patches and rouge, the set of her Majesty's head-dress, and the color of the Princess' gowns, have you been pondering over what I told you of my darling saint?"

"Yes," said Kate, with a little *malice* in her eyes; "but, dear madame, I cannot for the life of me think what so holy a soul could have had to say about herself; if it had been a reprobate like me now, 'twould have taken hours of the holy Bishop's time to convert me—and, to have me a saint, who would have grudged the time he lost? But beings like Madame de Chantal and Madame de Marigny, what can they have to say?"

The Duchesse took up a fan that lay near her, and threw it at Kate.

"Really, you are an incorrigible child! But a truce to nonsense: time is precious, and we have made no progress in our business. What do you think of this project of founding a Convent of the Visitation in England? Let each say what she thinks: Alethea, it is for you to begin."

Said Alethea:

"It is certain such a foundation is evidently desired by many, and numbers of subjects would enter. It seems to me that, if it were managed with due caution, the secret of its existence might be kept."

The Duchesse looked at Margery.

"Dear madame," said May, "it is the straits and difficulties that our dear Sisters of the Conception have to go through that a little frighten me. I know the nuns of the Visitation will be ready to endure any hardship and to risk their lives, but will they be able to keep their holy rule in any degree?"

"Perhaps not at first," answered the Duchesse; "but, in a little while, they will, for brighter times are at hand, dear friends. The King"—her voice involuntarily sank to a whisper, as if she feared the walls might bear—"the King is a Catholic in heart; if he dies, who succeeds him but James of York? and our own sweet Princess once on the throne, must win thousands of hearts to the cause."

"Yes," said Alethea, "my father was saying only the other day that, considering Mary Beatrice was but a child when she was married, and is only a young girl now, he expects great things from her in mature years, seeing how she has comported herself in early youth in difficult circumstances."

"Oh!" exclaimed May, with brightening face, "if this be so, what reason can there be against our project? It must bring God's blessing on the land; it must satisfy the longings of so many hearts who cannot for divers causes fly beyond seas."

"Now, Kate," cried the Duchesse, "what has the 'devil's advocate' to say against all this wise and weighty talk?"

Kate shook her head.

"Alas, dear madam, your hopes of better times for Catholics are not shared by all. Neither my father nor Father Whitbread takes a sangu'ne view of matters. It is true

the King is Catholic in heart, but what sort
of a heart has Charles? He believes the
truths of our holy faith, but he will sacrifice
for them not only not his crown, for that
were a goodly gift to lay before the Lord,
but not one of his sinful pleasures. Father
Whitbread said but a few days ago, in our
house at Kensington, 'So many prayers rise
up for Charles, so many noble hearts suppli-
cate for him with tears, that surely he shall
never be lost; but so hard is his heart, so
absorbed is he in selfish pleasures, that
methinks he shall be saved only, as the
Puritans are so fond of quoting, as a brand
from the burning.'"

"The King will not live forever," replied
the Duchesse, in a vexed tone (for while her
head acknowledged the force of Lady Katherine's reasoning, her heart was set on the
scheme she had proposed to Father de la
Colombière, and on which he had desired
her to consult her three friends).

"No," said Katherine, "but let us not
deceive ourselves—James is far from popular. Have you not heard the *bon mot* that
the King uttered the other day?"

"No," said the Duchesse; "I have no great love for the folly that comes from the royal lips."

"O, madame," cried Alethea, smiling, "you really are prejudiced! The King hath much wit. Surely you know the epitaph that Buckingham made for his Majesty, and repeated to his face. No!—it runs thus:

"'Here lies our sovereign lord the King,
    Whose word no man relies on ;
Who never said a foolish thing,
    Nor ever did a wise one.'"

"I never heard that before," said the Duchesse, laughing. "What an idea it gives one of Charles' utter forgetfulness of his dignity to allow such insolence to his face. Ciel! imagine anyone offering such an insult to his Majesty of France!"

"The Bastile for life, or his head chopped off, I trow would be his fate," remarked Alethea.

"There was a group of men at our house some months ago," said Kate, "and that epitaph was discussed. All agreed it exactly hit off the character of the King—clever, witty (good-hearted, as the world counts it), and entirely unreliable."

"Well, Kate, now let us have the wise saying of the King: we have digressed from it."

"It seems," replied Lady Katherine, "that some plot to kill his Majesty was afloat among the Puritans. The Duke heard of it, and warned his brother against their machinations. 'Well, no fear, James,' returned the King, laughing. 'They will never kill me to make you king.' When my father heard that, he sighed and said, ' 'Tis but too true!'"

"Well, then," said the Duchesse, in a disappointed tone, "you think this project impossible?"

"I do, in truth," exclaimed Kate.

"And you, Alethea? and you, Margery?"

"Not impossible, dear madame," answered Alethea, "but needing much thought and much prayer ere anything could be decided."

May was silent.

"That will not do, Margery," cried the Duchesse; "we are sitting in conclave: everyone must speak."

A deep flush overspread Margery's face.

"It seems presumptuous of me, but something seems to say to me the time has not yet come." Her eyes had a dreamy, far-off look, as of one who saw more than was visible to others, and she spoke in a low voice, as if impelled by some unseen power. "They will come; they *will* come: not the very first, but among the first; come in poverty, obscurity, in straits, but not till the sea be passed—the sea that lies between them and us."

She bent over her work again, and seemed absorbed in thought.

"What does she mean?" whispered Kate to the others; "of course they must cross the sea. Do we not live on an island?"

"There is a deeper meaning in her words than that," answered the Duchesse, in the same whispered tone. Then speaking aloud, she said, "Now for humility, and to own myself defeated. Our good Father is totally against my plan. He bade me not tell you so in the beginning, and, like all the saints, he is most humble, and distrusts his own lights. As I was so set upon this foundation, and as the wealth God hath given me could not be better bestowed than by the charge of such a house, he hath pondered over the matter, and he bade me call you three together, saying, with that bright smile of his you know so well, '*Four* heads are better than *two!*' Now see my willfulness and presumption to want to do something our good Father was averse unto."

"Oh!" cried Katherine, springing from her seat and holding up her hands in dismay, "if you, dear Duchesse, begin to confess in public, I shall have to do the same, and I love not that sort of work at all. Wait till you get into your convents, and do not drag a poor creature like me up the hill of such high perfection."

Ere any one could answer, there was a knock at the door, a lackey entered to say the coach of the Ladies Howard was ready, and, in a few moments, the friends separated.

CHAPTER XVII.

A STRANGE SURPRISE.

WHEN Lady Margery reached home
she found signs of commotion
in the house. Servants in those
days were not adepts in the art
of apparent impassibility as they are now,
and the lackeys cast wondering looks at
their young lady as she passed up the
grand staircase and entered her own apartment. She had hardly closed the door
before it was flung open, and Marguerite
entered. Was it Marguerite, or was it one
of the furies come to life from the tapestries?
Her eyes were flashing, her face and neck in
one crimson glow, her whole frame quivering
with emotion.

"May, have you heard?" she gasped, in a
low, hoarse tone.

May was pale as death.

"Oh, Rita, what is it? I have heard
nothing; our father, is he *dead?*"

"No," cried her sister, passionately, "better

if he were!" and, flinging herself on the
ground, she moaned as if in deep pain. In
her hand she held a letter, and, as May knelt
beside her with beating heart, longing to
hear more, yet not daring to question, Rita
thrust the letter towards her. May took it,
undid its scented folds, and read as follows:

"SWEETHEART—This letter shall bear you news,
but you will not, I think, mislike them. Your good
father will give me no peace till I consent to wed
him. Alas! it seemeth strangely soon to lay aside
my trappings of grief, but he brooks no delay. He
said with truth, my sweet girl, that you and my fair
Mayflower are left without a mother's care, and he
pleadeth with me to give it. My loved Marguerite,
my winsome pearl, shall shine as a gem in my
maternal crown; my daisy, so humble, my May-
blossom, so sweet, shall bloom by my side. What
happiness awaits us, *cherie*, to be one together under
one roof. At present, my place at court will be the
same. My lord sends you tender greeting. I
begged for a *congé* from her Highness, for your
father will carry me to Sheen, where we will abide
some days. Then we return to Pall Mall, not to
displace my sweet Marguerite, but to reign with
her. Your loving friend and mother,

"DIANA EDENHALL."

Such, in the stilted phraseology of the
time, ran Lady Diana's letter.

May was greatly shocked. That no one should ever fill her mother's place was a fixed idea in her mind. She had been taught it in her childhood, and believed it much as she believed that Charles II was the lawful King of England. But those who have learnt to overcome nature in the little things of daily life find their reward when they are in the midst of mental storms and earthquakes. They do not lose their balance; they are able to retain their reasoning powers. Their submission to the Divine will is like a mighty rock in the midst of falling ruins, under its shelter they are safe. May loved her father fondly, and the thought of a woman like Lady Diana occupying her mother's place was a sort of profanation in her eyes. Mother! that this false woman should dare to use the name; and then, in an instant, the childlike heart said its *fiat* and was at rest. The tears streamed down her face as she looked on her sister, crushed to earth with the blow.

May understood its bitterness to Marguerite. Hers was the sorrow that does the work of years. Life is not a succession of

days and nights; there are days and hours
that are the landmarks of our history.
Henceforth Marguerite's youth was over.
She might rise up and go forth in youth's
proud beauty, its fresh glow on her cheek,
its clear light in her eyes, but the heart,
hidden in the fair form, would have grown
old. The blue mists that make the distant
mountains look fairylike had melted away,
and the bare and stony hill was hurting her
feet. No more trust in honeyed words, in
fond embraces. She had often heard the
world was hollow, now she knew it. It was
true, though she could not feel it, that time
would pass on, and that she would trust
again to some extent; but it was also true,
though, she never would trust again with the
joyous *abandon* of her first love. Then Marguerite had lost her anchor. She had in
prosperity turned her back on God, and now,
in her sorrow, His Face was hidden from her.
Easy would it be to seek that Face again.
But poor Rita could not feel this. She raved
and moaned in horror and in grief against
the earthly instrument that had dealt the
blow, and she could not bend to the mighty
Power overruling all for her good.

"Rita, my own sister, speak to me; dearest love, how can I comfort you?"

"There is no comfort, May," said the hoarse voice, "only revenge!"

"Darling, do not say so."

"I will say it, and feel it, too. She has fooled me long enough; she has made me her slave; she has wrung and tortured my heart, and now this is the crown. Do you deem I shall submit? Do you dream she can sweep me from her path as she would an insect? I tell you no; she shall know all there is in Marguerite Clotilde Clymme."

Slowly she gathered herself up from the ground, and flung back her hair, which was falling in wild disorder.

"Oh, Rita," cried May, as she saw blood on her sister's face and dress, "you have hurt yourself; what is the matter?"

"Nothing," said Rita, impatiently; "I fell against a cabinet and cut my lip."

"Who brought you this letter?" inquired May. "How long have you had this sorrow to bear ere I returned?"

"I don't know," said Rita, putting her hand to her head wearily for physical pain was beginning to assert its mastery over mental anguish; "I had nothing to do after you went. I strolled into the Green Chamber, and began to examine that old black cabinet. I wanted to find out the secret drawer old Louise used to tell us of, that no one could discover who did not know the way to get at it. I believe I did find it out, and a musty old document tumbled into my lap. I was just going to read it when this letter came in, and, rising up, I fell against the edge of the cabinet."

"Why, you might have killed yourself, and it is quite a deep cut," said May, examining it. "Do let me tend on you, love; come to your own room and lie down, and I will bathe your face and comb your hair, as I always do when you are sick."

Rita was feeling sick and weak. She had tasted scarce any food that day. She allowed May to do as she liked. Together they entered the apartment, and, while May flew about settling pillows, and getting some water to wash her sister's face, the latter sank into a chair. But all May's cares availed little; the blood was stanched, and

Rita lay down, after having been persuaded to drink some wine and eat a morsel of bread; but she soon started up again, and paced restlessly up and down the room. At last she turned to her sister.

"May, go and fetch the paper that fell out of the secret drawer in the Green Chamber, and bring it me."

May gladly obeyed, hoping the manuscript might divert her sister's thoughts. On entering the Green Chamber, she saw Philip Engelby seated before the old cabinet, deeply engrossed in the contents of a dusty parchment, which looked very like that of which she was in quest. As May entered, he started up, a strange glitter was in his eyes, a dark red flush on his usually pale cheek.

CHAPTER XVIII.

THE GREEN CHAMBER.

AY stood still in astonishment, while Philip advanced towards her and cried, "Lady Margery, can I see your sister?" Unconsciously May drew herself up; her timidity never deprived her of her dignity.

"It is quite impossible, cousin. Lady Marguerite is very ill; she cannot leave her chamber."

"No wonder, no wonder!" exclaimed Philip, while his face darkened with anger; "'tis a base trick that hath been played on us, and your father hath been befooled."

"Master Engelby," said May, coldly, "I pray you to remember you speak in Lord Edenhal's house, and in the presence of his daughter."

"Cousin, I crave pardon," returned Philip; "the suddenness of this blow hath overset me."

"I know not why," said May, her cheeks flushing, "it should be a blow to you."

Philip was taken by surprise. For many months past he had looked on May as a soft, yielding child, an innocent *dévote*, whom any one could turn round his finger, and who took little heed of what was passing around. *Now* she stood looking at him with her clear, truthful eyes piercing the depths of his soul, and forcing him to reveal his hidden motives. He might deceive Marguerite; he could not deceive May.

She looked on a union between him and her sister as fraught with danger to the latter; and her courage rose to defend the being she so fondly cherished.

"You can hardly be ignorant," stammered Philip, "how long I have aspired to win your sister's hand."

"I know it," said May, "but I should have thought this—this—step of my father"—her voice faltered, but she recovered herself and went on steadily—"would have apparently made matters easier. It is true, my sister may not be a great heiress, but—"

"But that is the very point," burst in Philip. "See this very document which, by mere hazard, I have lighted on. O, I beseech

you, Lady Margery, let me see Marguerite.
It is of the utmost importance; even you
must feel it so, as a Catholic. I pray you let
me see your sister; bear her a message for
me."

"The document you hold," said May, with
increasing coldness, "is, if I mistake not, one
of ours. Suffer me to take it to my sister."

"Pardon: no! *I* would place it in her
own hands."

May looked her astonishment, but before
any more could be said the door was flung
open, and Marguerite entered.

She was pale as death, but her eyes were
glowing with feverish excitement. She had
attired herself hastily, and the disorder of
her dress formed a strange contrast to her
ordinary finished toilet. She advanced into
the room and sank into the nearest seat.

"What means all this parley?." she cried,
and, casting an indignant look at May, continued: "Am I to be treated like a child,
and kept in ignorance of some new phase of
this hideous plot?".

"No, dearest, fairest cousin," cried Philip,
thrusting the old parchment into her hands;

"by a lucky chance I found this. By its means you shall triumph indeed over this bad woman."

Marguerite unfolded the paper and looked along the dim lines, but she could not decipher them. Her head was swimming, and she grew ghastly pale.

" 'Tis a will," said Philip. " 'Tis the will of your grandfather. It was by his wife the Clymme estates came into your family. By this will they are left absolutely to the eldest daughter of his son. I know that it was always supposed such a will had been made and no one could find it. Your grandfather was, you know, killed in battle, and then, as his estates were sequestered, wills would have been of little avail. But now times are changed. Evidently this will has been hidden in some secret drawer. By what wonderful chance it cometh to light to-day, and I find it lying on the floor, it is more than I can tell."

"It was I," said Marguerite, in a fierce, hard tone; "I found it. To while away my time waiting for *her*, I played with the drawers of the cabinet. When we were chil·

dren our old nurse told us of a black cabinet in which there was a secret drawer. The paper was in my hands when the news came. Ha," continued she, while a strange, bitter smile glittered on her pale lips, "Providence is not so cruel as I deemed It. It leaves me yet revenge."

May drew near her sister, and put her arm around her. She had never in her life felt so strong a feeling of aversion as she now experienced for Philip. He was working upon the excited and wounded feelings of her sister in a state of physical weakness, and rousing her to a pitch of madness. She wished she dared call for help and send him away. She felt that terrible sensation of weakness that comes upon us when we are waging a battle with some power of evil; and then the habit of her life stood her in her need. She remembered the counsel of Father de la Colombière: "In all hours of anguish and peril, fly to the Heart of Jesus." Her soul fled to that sure place of refuge, and was still.

"Then," questioned Marguerite, eagerly, "I am at this moment the owner of the Clymme estates?"

"In another year, when you shall be of age," rejoined Philip; "but even now they should be held in trust for you. Your father hath had no right to enjoy their revenues during your childhood. All must be repaid. His new wife"—he spoke with a sort of hiss between his teeth—"will find she hath made a sorry bargain. She cannot reign over this grand mansion, and Edenhal, shorn of the Clymme property, will be but a mean dwelling for a countess."

"But surely," exclaimed May, "you will not persuade my sister to do this cruel wrong? My father never knew of this will; he hath believed the estates his own. Would you have his own child sue him for a debt an honorable stranger would not ask? Shame on you!"

Philip did not answer. He kept his eyes fixed on Rita. It seemed to May like a story she had read of a rattlesnake fascinating its victim ere it makes the spring.

Both waited for Marguerite to speak again. The words came slowly.

"Had he been true to me, had he treated me as a child hath a right to be treated, he should scarce have known this. Had he chosen to wed again—I have no right to gainsay him—he should only have known of this to guide him for the future. I mean had he wedded in the light of day, and one who would not disgrace the name we bear. But, when he hath joined in a plot against me, when he hath misled and befooled me, shall I have mercy, shall I spare? Great heaven, no!"

She clasped her hands, and the wild anguish of her face might have moved many a heart to pity.

"Write that down, sweetest cousin," Philip cried. "See, here is paper. I will write it for you in an instant, and you have but to sign it."

He turned away to an adjacent writing-table and began his task.

"But why this haste?" demanded May. "'Tis most unseemly haste. We have friends we would consult, and there can be no need whatever of such hurry."

She received no answer. Marguerite lay back in her chair with closed eyes. Philip wrote on rapidly. May also closed her eyes,

and cried earnestly within her heart,
"Domine, ad adjuvandum me festina."

Philip sprang from his seat, and brought
the paper to Marguerite. He placed a pen
within her fingers, but it fell upon her lap;
her eyes did not open. She had fainted.

Instantly May threw open the door and
called for assistance. She pointed at Philip
with an imperative gesture, and he obeyed.
A sense that to be found in his present position would not be advantageous for the future
flashed upon him. He thrust the will into
his pocket, and, before the servants could
reach the room, had made his exit by another
door.

CHAPTER XIX.

RITA'S TRIAL.

T last that terrible day was over. Marguerite, exhausted by all she had gone through, was at last persuaded to go to bed, and, after tossing about restlessly, moaning with pain, for several hours, sank into a deep sleep as the morning began to dawn.

Leaving her to be watched by a servant she could trust, May stole over to the palace to hear Mass.

After it was over, she sought Father de la Colombière. He was startled at the pale, wan face of one whom he had seen only the previous day bright and blooming.

May had not slept—she had passed the night in prayer by her sister's side, and the emotions of the previous day had left their mark upon her. She told her tale, and Father de la Colombière listened with deep interest.

One of his characteristics was a deep

sympathy for the sorrow of others. Rare is
the gift; blessed are those who possess it.
To them is committed a power of healing
the wounds of the soul to a degree that seems
miraculous. Their words are few and simple,
but they never sound like platitudes. They
can probe a wound, and the sufferer does not
wince. They can reprove, yet their words
leave no bitterness behind.

Such was Father de la Colombière; such
was the secret of that wondrous charm which
drew so many in England to his feet.

"This is, indeed, a heavy cross for you, my
dear child," he said to Margery. "I know
no one to whom a marriage, such as that
between your sister and Philip Engelby,
would be more injurious than to Lady Marguerite. If she marries, her husband should
be a man she both loves and respects."

"And, Father, with Philip she can do
neither. She cannot respect him. I feel
certain she loves him not."

"While," continued the Father, "he is a
man without religion, without principle. I
cannot imagine a more dreadful fate. Let
us try to save her from it, my child. If she

is sick and unable to leave the house, I will come to her. Then, I think, her Highness has some influence over her. Speak to Mary Beatrice, without delay, of the matter. It were well, I think, if you and your sister came to your apartment in the palace, even though you are not on duty just now. Surely it will not be well for Lady Marguerite and the new Countess to meet under one roof."

"I had thought of that, Father; but you know Lady Diana still keeps her place at court—we shall be in constant contact."

"Oh, my child, that can't be avoided. Besides, do not imagine for a moment I would counsel you to keep up an estrangement. You must not fail in respect for your father. He has a perfect right to wed a second time. It is only the peculiar circumstances of the case which render it a blow to you both, but especially to your sister. I would counsel you to write to your father to day a dutiful epistle. Before doing so, see her Highness; she will, I am sure, bid you return to the palace, and you can say to your father you have done so by her wish. Let me have news of Lady Marguerite in a few hours; and, last of all, my child," continued he, with a smile, "*you* must not fall sick."

May dashed away a few tears, and answered him with a bright smile. She was able to bear her burden better now. No one who sought Father de la Colombière's help in faith ever went away unconsoled. He had the art of raising the drooping spirit, and inspiring the faint-hearted with hope and courage.

When May returned home she found Rita awake, and, though very ill, determined on moving to the palace. In the course of the day the transit was accomplished. Philip Engelby called, but as his name was brought to Margery, she was able to dismiss him with an assurance that her sister was too ill to see him; and when Marguerite had accomplished the brief journey from Pall Mall to the palace, she became so much worse that for several days she was unable to attend to anything passing around. By her side May watched and prayed. Willingly would Alethea or the Duchesse de Marigny have shared her labors, but Rita shrank from a strange voice or step.

Lord Edenhall brought back his wife to Pall Mall, and May went to receive them. It was a formal, constrained interview, and both parties were glad when it was over. Lady Edenhall seemed fatigued, and complained of a headache. Few inquiries were made for Marguerite. Evidently her illness was felt as a sort of relief. It broke the ice of their first meeting.

The Countess was not sorry that her stepdaughter had retreated to the palace, and that she was left alone to carry out the schemes of pride and pleasure in her new domain.

But at Marguerite's age grief does not kill, not even crush. The wound in her heart healed, the fever in her veins abated, and she rose up from her bed to face life again.

She was greatly changed. It was extraordinary to see the inroads that sickness and grief had made on her beauty. Her manner was cold and hard and defiant. She scorned sympathy—dashed affection from her. She would not see Father de la Colombière—would listen to no message from him. She never opened a prayer book or looked at a crucifix.

The Duchess of York came to visit her, and Marguerite could not refuse her royal mistress; but Mary Beatrice found her cold and reserved. The Duchess was of too timid a nature to contend with Marguerite; and when she found the loving sympathy she was ready to offer met by stately ceremony, as if there could be no relation possible with her maid-of-honor save that of mistress and servant, she felt repelled, and was glad to end the visit.

But as soon as Marguerite was able to rise she sent for Philip Engelby, and had a long interview with him. One of her English maids attended upon her, and the conversation between Marguerite and Philip was carried on in French.

She said nothing of what had passed to anyone; and, as far as May knew, the mystery of the will found in the Green Chamber remained unknown to Lord and Lady Edenhall.

CHAPTER XX.

IN THE PALACE GARDEN.

IT was a few days after the secret conference between Marguerite and Philip; night had closed in; the noise and stir of a large household had died away; all had retired to rest, and Father de la Colombière was, as usual, rapt in prayer before the Tabernacle, when he was startled by a low knock at his door. A little boy stood on the threshold, who bore a note.

Father de la Colombière unfolded it, and read the following lines in Margery's handwriting:

"FATHER—Rita is going. In half an hour it will be too late. Laure has only just discovered it. They are to meet in the garden; he has by some means procured a key to a side-gate. She will fly with him and be married by the Protestant rite. Oh, Father, save her! Laure and I are waiting for you in the garden; the side-door by the fountain is open. Dismiss this child."

With a few kind words, the child was sent away.   Father de la Colombière wrapped himself in his cloak, drew a low Spanish hat over his brows, and descended to the garden. At the spot appointed, he met Margery and her waiting-maid, the former pale and trembling. She pointed to a tree at some distance from them, where stood two closely-veiled and muffled figures. They were Marguerite and her attendant.

Just as May and her two companions reached this spot, Philip Engelby, with rapid steps, entered the garden from a side-gate, and approached the party, saying,

"There is no time to be lost, Rita."

He started back as he saw the intruders.

"Ha! what means this?" he cried.

"That you cannot take Lady Marguerite Clymme at this unseemly hour from those who are bound to protect her," said Father de la Colombière.

"Mon Père," exclaimed Marguerite, "I pray you do not interfere. I am mistress of my own actions. I go with my cousin and future husband by my own free act and will."

"Hearest thou what the lady says?" said Philip, his face darkening with rage. "We want no spiritual fooling and priestly domination here. Stand back, Monsieur l'Aumônier, or by Heaven I'll make you repent it!"

"I shall not yield," said the priest. "I am parleying thus only to shield Lady Marguerite's name from scandal; but, if you do not instantly withdraw, and allow her to regain her chamber in safety, I will alarm the household."

Philip paused for a moment as if irresolute. Father de la Colombière turned his gaze on Marguerite, to see the effect of his words; but Margery's eyes were fixed on Philip.

The priest moved nearer to Marguerite. In an instant something glittered in the moonlight. May threw herself upon his arm. A low cry burst from her lips, and a gush of warm blood welled from her side. The blow aimed at the Father had struck the faithful child.

With a gasp of horror, Marguerite started forward and caught her sister in her arms. Philip, not even yet losing his self-possession, whispered to Marguerite,

"Leave her to her maid, and fly. In the confusion we shall escape."

Marguerite did not answer even by a glance. With sobs of anguish she hung over the apparently lifeless form, while Father de la Colombière, assisted by Laure and Victoire, endeavored to stanch the life-blood that was ebbing fast away.

Muttering a curse, Philip bit his lip, and turned away. "The game is up," said he, between his teeth, as he let himself out at the garden gate.

Victoire succeeded in bandaging the wound, and then Laure, a strong, vigorous woman, lifted May's light form in her arms and carried her towards the palace. There was a sort of unspoken consent among the four actors in this strange scene to keep the occurrence, if possible secret. They had been standing upon soft earth, and the rain which was beginning to fall would soon efface all evidence of the fray.

Father de la Colombière regained his room unobserved, changed his dress, and anxiously awaited a summons to Lady Margery's chamber.

In about an hour came the expected knock, and Monsieur Bonjean, the little, fat, good-natured French doctor to the Duchess of York, entered.

"What, up again, mon Père?" said he, rubbing his hands; "if all the world thought as little of their lives as you do, my occupation would be gone. I have come to tell you that Lady Margery Clymme is very ill."

"Indeed!" said the Father, "that is very sudden!"

"Very much so," returned the doctor; "stabs in the side have not, as far as I know, any premonitory symptoms. Now, sir," continued the little man, dropping his tone of banter, "I can keep a secret, if need be, as well as a priest. Lady Margery did not stab herself; that is certain from the position of the wound. Neither do I think the little angel that she is would tell a lie to save a life. 'Tis a wonderful creature that! With those great eyes of hers fixed on you with a pleading look, a man feels he must do what she asks, and not cross her. Well, when I had dressed her wound and bade her lie still, she would speak to me alone. Then.

stretching forth her hand, she said, 'Doctor,
you will keep this secret?' I answered,
'Chère demoiselle, a man cannot hold his
tongue and see foul wrong without opening
his lips. You are too generous. Your
father is bound to punish this midnight
assassin. I know you do not want the court
to ring with your name, but Lord Edenhall
must know.' 'If Père de la Colombière
agrees with me, will you consent?' she said.
'Yes,' I replied; 'I will leave the matter to
his decision.' 'Go, then, to him,' she said;
'he will tell you all, and pray him to come
to me when the morning breaks. I shall
live till then, shall I not?' I nearly
answered that she would live to laugh at her
adventure, but someway the words stuck in
my throat. I could not deceive those truthful eyes. So I simply answered, 'There is
no pressing danger if you obey my direc-
tions;' and I hastened here."

"Then there is no hope?" demanded
Father Colombière.

"None whatever," replied the doctor.
"She has had her deathblow. She will not
do more than get through the day that is

dawning this very Friday on which we have entered."

"The first Friday of the month," said Father de la Colombière to himself, in a low tone; and then he told Monsieur Bonjean the whole story.

"I see," exclaimed the doctor, when it was finished; "we must not drag Lady Marguerite's name through the mud. A precious rascal that fellow must be! I should like to wring his neck. Well, well, there will be another angel in heaven before night. I do not know but that is the only fit place for such as that fair flower. She is not meant for this world's gibes and turmoil. We must say it is bleeding at the lungs, and conceal the rest, I suppose."

So saying, he rose, and wished Father de la Colombière farewell.

CHAPTER XXI.

PARTING.

THE day passed on, and the gentle life of Margery Clymme was passing with it. The Duchesse de Marigny and Alethea Howard watched by her side. Merry Kate Howard came, with beating heart and swollen eyes, to press a last kiss on the pale brow. Mary Beatrice wept over the attendant she had fondly loved. Beside the bed knelt Marguerite, immovable to all save the sufferer. Not a word, not a look, did she lose. She hung upon each syllable, she treasured up each glance. The love of their childhood, the affection of their riper years, which had seemed to be dried up and withered in her heart, sprang forth in new life and vigor. No one dared to disturb her; no one, save Father de la Colombière, ventured to speak to her, and he addressed her in few words. He knew the hour for human help and consolation had not yet come; God was doing His own work in that agonized soul.

The Father spent much time in the sick chamber; but more than once the sisters were left alone. May could not speak often, for the loss of so much blood had brought on great exhaustion; but the watchers in the adjoining chamber knew that she spoke to Marguerite. They could hear the low tones and the smothered answer.

Neither Lord nor Lady Edenhall came to break the peace of this death-scene. They were at Edenhall for a few days, and the swiftest courier could not let them know in time.

"'Twas a pity," said the Ladies Howard and the Duchess.

"That dying saint," exclaimed Kate, "might convert harder hearts than even the stern Earl and the worldly Countess."

"She lies there, looking like a broken lily," sobbed Alethea; "what shall I do without her?"

Oh, cry of anguish that has burst from so many hearts in this dreary vale of tears! Blessed are those of whom it is said. It tells the certain tale that they have done their work, that they have comforted the hearts of others, and shed a bright light of example amidst the weary maze of this world.

The belief that May was a saint had for long been growing up in the minds of her intimate friends. She spoke little on spiritual subjects, and her life was unmarked by any extraordinary action. But sanctity is an atmosphere, and in it May dwelt.

Well, she was dying now, and still her words were few, her actions simple. There was nothing thrilling or exciting around that death-bed. A stranger would have deemed May did not know she was dying. But she knew it well; only, for *her*, death had no fears. She was going to Him in whom her life had been hidden, on whom all her thoughts were set, to whom she had given her heart.

But May was a child of earth, and even her death was not without its sufferings. She was a follower of the Crucified, and she must needs feel the shadow of His Cross. He had to part from His sinless Mother; May had to bid farewell to her erring sister.

"O May," wailed Rita, "do not leave me! Too late I know what you are to me. The

glamor is gone; the devil is cast out. Could
I dwell by your side, I should be safe.
Without you, what can become of me? O
May, ask God to let you stay!"

Father de la Colombière was in the room.
May turned her pleading eyes to him, and he
answered the mute question in these words·

"She shall be my special care. As long
as God suffers me, I will never forsake her."

"Life is short, Rita, love," said· the dying
girl; "and to me it seems but a day since
mine began. Yours will soon pass, and we
shall be together—forever."

Her voice grew weak. A sudden grey
shade crept over her·face.

Father de la Colombière made a sound
which brought in Alethea, the Duchesse,
Laure and Victoire. He began the prayers
for the dying, and the women responded.

Early in the. day May had been anointed
and· had received the Viaticum. Prayers
were all she needed to help her in her pas-
sage home. As Henriette de Marigny and
Alethea looked up, they fancied they could
almost see the bright company of angels
coming to meet her; they could almost hear

the choir of virgins singing jubilees who were to receive her. Did May see them, hear them, too? Or were her wondering eyes fixed on a greater sight? They were open wide, like a child's that sees for the first time some marvellous and beauteous spectacle. A look of astonished rapture transformed her face. The color came into her cheeks. Her hands dropped the crucifix and were locked together. Yea, Margery, oft hast thou meditated on Him; oft hast thy heart pictured His "mild and festive aspect." Those thoughts were shadows; this is the reality. Thy eyes have seen the King in His beauty. Thou hast entered the land that is very far off.

Lord and Lady Edenhall returned to London with all speed, and their first meeting with Marguerite took place in the chamber of death. Nothing could induce Marguerite to quit the corpse. She never slept, and never tasted any food, save a few drops Mary Beatrice herself, standing by her, cup in hand, compelled her to swallow.

Margery was most beautiful in death. A smile hovered on her lips, and her features looked as if they were chiselled in ivory. A crucifix was between her clasped hands, and on her breast lay a little picture she had drawn herself, of the Saviour opening His side and showing His Sacred Heart. She was, in all probability, the first person on whose death-cold breast the image of the Heart of burning love, her refuge in life, her rest in death, was laid.

By the side of the corpse sat Marguerite, nearly as pale and as silent as her dead sister.

Many wondered that Lady Edenhall came at all. She was known not to be fond of being brought face to face with death. The truth was, she wanted to get over her first interview with Marguerite, and she thought it would be easier to do it on an occasion when both would be under a sort of unwonted excitement, and when surrounding circumstances would make the change in their relative positions less obvious.

Marguerite endured her father's kisses, though she never answered him when he asked kindly after her health, and never rose to her feet. But, when his wife approached, her eyes flashed fire, and Lady Edenhall, cowed for once in her life, drew back.

The suddenness of May's death did not excite much surprise. It had somehow been said she had broken a blood-vessel on her lungs; and people repeated this, while no one could trace the quarter whence the report sprang. May had always been a fragile creature, and her untimely ending, therefore, was looked upon without surprise. Lord Edenhall made a few inquiries of her maid, and seemed satisfied.

Lady Edenhall was anxious to get away. As she entered the corridor, she met Father de la Colombière so suddenly that involuntarily the priest raised his eyes; and his glance of deep compassion fell on the Countess. He started back as a look of dark burning hatred answered him.

"Yes," she said, in low tones, "I have done wisely to escape the snares in which you have entangled those poor girls. One lies there a victim to your power; the other, I suppose, will follow in her steps. Doubtless," she sneered, "you think the sight of the pale corpse decked out with flowers, and with some horrible picture lying on her bosom, would move me to repentance. Pardon,

Monsieur l'Aumônier, I am not so easily caught. Hear me," she continued, in hard, eager tones; " by that dead girl I vowed that I will drive you from the palace. This cursed devotion you practice shall not gain ground in this free land. Beware, beware in time. Yield, or my vengeance is sure."

Lord Edenhall's step was heard in the distance approaching, yet she looked eagerly in the priest's face for an answer. But the Father did not reply to her. He only said, in a low tone,

"I will fear no evils, for Thou art with me."

CHAPTER XXII.

LIGHT AND STRENGTH.

WHEN the time came to remove the mortal remains of Lady Margery to their last resting-place, Marguerite's grief became uncontrolable. No change had passed on May's lovely features. Still lingered the smile upon the half-parted lips. "Death's effacing finger" had not begun its work. To Marguerite, as it has been to many others, the removal of the corpse was a fresh separation; or, rather, it was not till then she realized she had lost for ever in this world the truest friend, the most tender love she was ever likely to know.

A mighty anguish overpowered her. It was the hour in her life when the dark waters entered into her soul. She flung herself upon the lifeless body, and, in delirious tones, implored May to speak, to come back to life, not to leave her, to forgive her, not to leave the keen darts of remorse forever to rankle within her breast. The gentle tones of Henriette and Alethea had no power over her.

The funeral cortege had assembled, and the attendants to carry away the corpse were already in the corridor. Alethea sent for Père de la Colombière. He entered the room, and with a few words contrived to gain ascendency over Marguerite so far as to induce her to allow the servants to enter and perform the last sad offices.

When the corpse of Margery Clymme was carried out, the Father's hand was raised in benediction. She was laid in ground consecrated long before; but the cold ritual of an alien creed was read over her grave. She recked it not. Unseen angels hovered round chanting the prayers of Holy Church. Angel hands poured down upon her the Church's benedictions. Those who were with her were mightier than those who were against her. To worldly eyes her early death, her hurried sepulture, so different from that of other daughters of her noble line, seemed as a misery. But she was numbered with the children of God, her lot was among the saints.

Down the corridor echoed the tread of the funeral train. The Duchesse, the Ladies Howard, and the servants followed it to the palace gates. Marguerite was left alone with the Father. She had sunk on a couch, for her tottering limbs could not sustain her weight. Father de la Colombière sat down beside her and spoke.

We can record but few of his words. Were we to tell them all, they would be deemed striking and beautiful, but we could have no idea of the force with which they went to the almost broken heart of Marguerite.

Father de la Colombière was a man of great tenderness of heart and of deep feeling, both rigidly governed by his habitual self-control. The rule of St. Ignatius, which is like a fire that burns up the dross of natural impulses, and purifies to marvellous perfection the powers of the soul, was not enough for this ardent being. He had long since bound himself by vow to do that which is more perfect. When, therefore, a nature like his exerts its utmost strength to comfort a sorrowing or to raise up a desponding soul, it is rare indeed that it fails. "Like rivers of water in a dry place, like the shadow of a great rock in a weary land," came the message of the Lord to Marguerite by the lips of His servant.

Hitherto she had known little of Father. de la Colombière. In the days of her thoughtless gaiety she had avoided him; and when they had met he had confined himself to speaking a few kind words. With his keen discernment he had seen that the hour of his ministry to this soul had not yet come. During these past days of anguish he had purposely left her alone to wrestle with her God. Instead of speaking to her he had prayed for her. But now the time was come and he spoke. In low, calm tones, his eyes fixed on a crucifix, he spoke, and, like St. Paul of old, the scales fell off the blinded eyes of Rita. She saw the folly of the past; she saw also the infinite love that had waited for her. She saw how the thorns and briers with which she had entangled herself had wounded the Hands that were ever seeking her. Her heart was well-nigh broken, because in her defence May's young blood had flowed. She saw how freely for her a more precious Life-Blood had been shed, over which she had never dropped a tear.

Father de la Colombière's words had not to pierce a stony rock. Marguerite's was not a nature incrusted with worldliness, dead to the instincts of faith. *Now* the patient toil of the obscure nun in the Faubourg St. Jacques was to bear its fruit. *Now* the faith of her childhood woke up in all its vigor. Prayers said in obedience, Sacraments which seemed like routine, found living voices, and said, "Behold our fruit, hidden for many a day, but not wasted or consumed."

A mighty change was wrought in that poor soul. The bitterness of her wild remorse was changing into that sorrow which in itself is peace. Henriette de Marigny looked into the room and withdrew in awe.

Father de la Colombière did indeed look like the picture she had often imagined of Him to whose feet the broken-hearted were wont to creep and be at rest.

"Despair not, my child," went on the low, calm voice; "this day is the beginning of a better life for you; sorrow not for her who is gone, and who has exchanged earth's sufferings for an eternal weight of glory. I, who knew her inmost soul, can say, with all but certainty, that she is among the saints in bliss. Her love was but the shadow of the love whose sweetness you shall know. She has bequeathed to you as a legacy her boundless love for Jesus. It was her life, the secret of her brightness, her influence, her peace. Her sole earthly desire for herself was to consecrate herself to Him in religion; but He took her by a shorter road to lie on His Sacred Heart. As the Christians of old were baptized in blood, so, by suffering and sacrifice, that dear child won the spousal ring from her Beloved."

When at last Father de la Colombière left Marguerite, she submitted to Henriette de Mariguy like a little child.

The Duchesse remained with her for a few days at the palace, while they went through the last sad task of gathering up all May's belongings, of breaking all the links of the life that had now ended for the two sisters.

During those few days, Marguerite knelt at the altar where May had so often received the Bread of Life, never without praying that her twin sister might soon be at her side again.

There is a superstition that the death of one twin saps the fullness of life in the other. Be there truth or not in the saying, Marguerite was changed from that funeral day, so utterly that none could know her. After a few days, the Duchesse de Marigny took her to her own house, and tried her utmost to revive her broken spirits and repair her shattered health.

But weeks and months passed on, and the bright Marguerite did not come back. Another creature altogether rose from her ashes, in whose eyes dwelt a deep peace, and on whose face suffering had left its traces.

She was willing to return to her father's house, but Lady Edenhall did not choose it. She called on her stepdaughter once at the Duchesse's house, intending to try her utmost to regain her ascendency over her. But she found the Rita she sought dead and buried in the grave of her twin sister, and Marguerite, "silent and serene," was not to her taste.

Thus, when Marguerite craved leave of her father to "go beyond seas," Lady Edenhall urged him to grant the request. The thought of her escaped victim troubled her; and, unable to conquer, she wanted to get her out of her sight. So there was no opposition; and, on one lovely morning in the summer of 1678, three companions—Henriette de Marigny, Alethea Howard and Marguerite—set sail for France, intending to bend their steps to the little town of Paray-le-Monial.

CHAPTER XXIII.

MILADI SCHEMES.

ADY EDENHALL was sitting in the retiring-room of her house in Pall Mall. It had served the same purpose for her stepdaughter; but, in their time, its appointments were simple; now every luxury known and invented was lavished around.

But the Countess, as she sat at her writing-table, did not look like a person happy or at ease. She had changed much for the worse since we first made her acquaintance. Her manners had grown haughty and arrogant; her beauty was on its wane; and the artificial helps she used for its preservation were becoming more and more evident. There was a restless fire in her eyes, a twitching of her lips, that told of inward disquiet.

She was examining various papers which lay on her table with much eagerness; but, as she finished the perusal of one after another, she flung them down with an impatient gesture.

"Nothing there," she muttered, as she finished the last; "he is too cunning to betray himself. Verily, I have spent much gold for naught. It costs a heavy sum to bribe the *femme de chambre* of a princess to steal letters from her private casket, and 'tis provoking to think I can find nothing. I don't think a word of these could be twisted into a plot against his Majesty, nor yet an attempt to introduce Papistry again into this land. The Reverend Father confines himself most scrupulously to the direction of her Highness's conscience, and these letters would only be evid.nce that he does *not* mix himself up with State affairs. Ha, ha! I see his Reverence does not like her Highness's weakness for cards. It shall be my daily task to foster and encourage that tendency in Mary Beatrice. She obeys him, doubtless, by never asking for a card-party; but, when we begin the sport, she cannot resist joining in it; and, if well plied, as I know how to do it, will play for high stakes. Then I know now the secret of her downcast look when the game is over. And—odd I thought it—after the first moment of exultation, she is as vexed when she has won as when she has lost. I see now she dreads an admonition; for this wily Jesuit tells her that money thus gained makes but sorry alms, and a penny given as the result of self-denial will bring more blessing than a hundred gold angels, which are the fruit of self-indulgence. Pshaw! I hate such folly. The man is a hypocrite. I cannot, I will not, believe he can live the life of an owl, as he does, willingly. There must be something behind the scenes. Are we not all acting a part, and why should he alone be walking the paths of truth and simplicity?"

There was a low tap at the door.

"*Entrez*," said the Countess.

A servant, entering and bowing low, said,

"The young man who was here yestereven craves speech of your honored ladyship."

"Bid him enter," she exclaimed; and in a few instants Arsène, whose interview with Father de la Colombière our readers have not forgotten, entered the room. He was no longer the shabby-looking individual who presented himself before the priest. Well dressed, and evidently well-off in other respects, was this genteel young man. He made a most lowly obeisance to the Countess, and stood hat in hand awaiting her orders.

"Well, Arsène," she began, "I grieve to say 'tis all useless so far. After the labor and expense of procuring these letters, they prove nothing—absolutely nothing!"

"Ah, indeed, miladi; be not cast down; I have long felt that looking for proofs against this kind of folks is useless. They are fools more than knaves. Dangerous fools, I grant, and to be got rid of; but as to seeking *true* accusations against them, save and except the Papistry forbidden by law, which undoubtedly they practice, it is impossible."

"And do you mean to tell me they are not hypocrites?" demanded the Countess.

"Miladi, if they are, their acting surpasses that of anyone seen on this earth. When I dwelt among them in the little lodging I told you of in the city, I watched and waited with all my skill to catch them out in somewhat, but in vain. They spent their time in prayer and study. When they were together, which occurred but rarely, or when some one who dwelt at a distance came to see them, there was talk and laughter. Oftentimes I contrived to listen at the door, and I found peals of laughing were caused by the stories of the disguises they had adopted, or the hairbreadth escapes they had sustained. How one had gone about like a miller, with a sack of flour on his back, and even now his hair was whitened. How another had, when the alarm of a search was raised in a house where he was tarrying, gone into the kitchen and turned scullion."

"Well, well," cried Lady Edenhall, "for what purpose did they thus stoop? For what end did they run these risks? There is the point. There must be some political reason."

"No, miladi, I believe it not. They are content, these strange beings, to eat the dust, to risk their rest, their goods, their heads even, to say Mass. That was the one story of these days I tell you of. They say Mass at dead of night, in forest huts or city cellars. In these efforts their lives seem to consist, their hearts to abide."

"Is it then hopeless, Arsène?" cried

Diana, springing from her seat and pacing
the room with restless steps, like a tigress
deprived of her prey. "I have sworn to be
revenged on this man. I have plotted for it
for months. Are he and the whole of this
detestable crew to escape? Are you such a
coward you can devise nothing?"

"Pardon, miladi. Your revenge is sure.
I have only said that by *true* accusations we
shall never succeed. There always remains
to us the *false.*"

Lady Edenhall seated herself again without
a word.

"You know, miladi," pursued Arsène,
speaking in a familiar tone no other inferior
would have dared to use with her, "there is
no use blistering one's tongue with lies; so
why should I go on telling them to your
honored ladyship? But, miladi, before this
year runs out, nay, perhaps in a few days, a
plot that hath been hatched by one Master
Oates—mark the name well, miladi—will
burst forth, and let every Papist in England
tremble, for h's or her doom is sealed."

"Say you so, veritably?" said Diana.

"I swear it, miladi. All we want is gold."

"Take it," exclaimed she, pushing a purse towards him; "count the contents; I warrant 'tis more than a hundred angels."

As Arsène stooped over the table to count the gold, a letter fell from his pocket. The handwriting caught Lady Edenhall's eye, and she grasped the letter.

"Ha, Arsène, I know the writer of this. Are you in communication with him? Lie not to me; he also is my enemy."

"I will not lie, miladi. I know Master Engelby is not devoted to your honored ladyship; but I also know that all other feelings are swallowed up in the vehement hate he bears to the chaplain at St. James'. He is heart and soul with us, helping on this plot of which I speak. Your ladyship knows he has no *gold* to spare."

"'Tis true. Poor Philip!" She mused for a moment. "Think you, Arsène, he would use this diamond if I sent it him?" and, so saying, she took from a little box beside her an unset stone of great value.

"Surely, miladi. He will be honored by such a gift, and forget any unreasonable wrath he hath cherished against you."

"Ah, Arsène, if you could do *that*, if you could bring about a good understanding between us, a rich guerdon and my undying thanks shall be yours. Go, now, my good youth, and hasten to me again when you have news to give."

Arsène again bowed low, and, gathering up his spoils, withdrew.

CHAPTER XXIV.

THE SEED SCATTERED.

E have more than once, in the course of this history, paid a visit to the little convent hidden in the Grange near May Fair; but we have not had time to enter more minutely into the lives of its holy inmates, or describe the abundant work they were doing for God's greater glory. Not only were their constant prayers and penances rising up to heaven, but their days were filled with good deeds.

The suffering endured by poor Catholics in those days was intense. In order to have a chance of practicing their religion, of bringing up their children in the faith, they had often to refuse prospects of advancement and keep themselves in obscure poverty. Were they the objects of spite and envy on the part of others, there was no redress. If they went to law, they knew an exposure of their Faith would be the result. To such as these, the Nuns of the Conception brought relief. They made garments for the destitute; they fed a number of children who managed to thread their way through the winding paths, the trees and the brushwood, which made the Grange so safe a hiding-place. When necessary, the nuns would leave their convent, and go forth to visit the sick and dying.

Their distance from the city, where most of the poorer Catholics were congregated, was a great drawback; and often, with blistered feet and weary bodies, did the nuns return from their walks, or, rather, scrambles, over the rough and muddy streets of London. But they were willing to endure all hardships for their Master's sake; and, moreover, they were sanguine—they thought better times were at hand, and that they would soon be able to emerge from their present dwelling, and establish themselves in the heart of the city. These pleasing anticipations were soon to be rudely dispelled.

The community were gathered together at their simple dinner, when a hurried knock was heard at the door. It was opened, and

Katherine Howard hastily entered. Her face wore traces of deep grief; she was trembling from head to foot.

"Dearest heart!" exclaimed the Mother Superior, "what ails you?"

Some of the Sisters drew her into a seat, for she was gasping for breath.

"My father," she said, "is in prison, and a crowd of other gentlemen. Father Whitbread is taken, and many others of the society, and numerous priests besides. A fearful plot or conspiracy is set on foot against us, and, it is said, we shall all be destroyed from the land. Oh, my Alethea, thanks be to God thou art safe in thy convent home! And you, Sisters, must fly."

"Fly!" said the Superior. "Alas, must this indeed be our fate? Are we not counted worthy to endure the prison-cell, the torture, and even death, to win a martyr's crown?"

"I bear you Father de la Colombière's own advice; for the present he is safe; indeed, I suppose they will not dare to touch her Highness's chaplain."

"Ah," said Sister Magdalene Lacy, "they

drove away Père St. Germain, although he
held the same post."

"Yes, but then he was conspired against,"
remarked Mother Elizabeth. "Let us hope
no such villainy will be exercised towards
this good Father, this apostle of the Sacred
Heart. But, dearest Kate, what can we do
to comfort you? Is there nothing in our
power?"

"No, dear Mother and Sisters," said Kate,
gradually regaining her composure; "we
have but to part—and, I fear, forever in
this world. You must fly with all speed,
and I shall never rest till I have joined my
father in his prison."

"Kate, do not be cast down," said Sister
Agnes; "I cannot but think your father
will escape. Why, 'twill be a shame before
the world if Lord Stafford's gray hairs be
touched. Take heart, dear Kate; we poor
nuns are different; we are pestilent, indeed,
in past-time merrie England, and, if our
hiding-place be discovered, we had best be
gone."

"Thanks, dear Sisters all," said Kate, "for
your cheering words. My poor heart says

you nay—but I count on your prayers, dear
ones. Pray for him continually that he may
do God's holy will, and I have patience to
stand beneath His cross and forgive those
who have torn his gray head away from my
loving arms—he who hath been upright in
all his dealings, who hath been a father to
the poor, a friend to the fatherless and the
widow; and so these days are over. How
often have Alethea and I passed happy hours
here; how often we come hither with Margery! Ah, she hath escaped this evil, and
hath fled like a bird out of the fowler's hand.
Adieu, adieu, dear Sisters; I must not
tarry;" and so saying she embraced each of
the community in turn, and, striving to stem
her tears, hastened from the room.

The nuns immediately set about their
simple preparations for departure, but they
could not leave the spot until some priest
should come and remove the Blessed Sacrament; at least they would try to procure one
before venturing on the extraordinary step
of concealing in their own faithful breasts
the hidden God. In the course of the day
they contrived to send a message to St

James' Palace, and also to arrange with the captain of a trading vessel then lying in the Thames to take them on board the following evening. Their messenger to the palace returned with an answer; and when the first gray light of dawn was piercing the heavens, Père de la Colombière made his way across the silent, deserted May Fair, through the scattered trees of the farm. All was ready for the Mass, and never had the nuns assisted with more awe at the Holy Sacrifice, for he who offered it seemed more like a seraph than a man. Each Sister received Holy Communion. The Bread of Angels was consumed —the Tabernacle was empty—it was another upper chamber, and these faithful hearts were ready to go forth in the strength of that meat to their Gethsemane and Calvary.

For some time after Mass, Père de la Colombière; knelt in silence; all around him were praying also, and with an intensity of supplication and vehement confidence into which we, nursed in the lap of security—we, too soft to make heroic sacrifices—cannot enter.

At last he rose and turned towards the

Community; his face was glowing with anearthly radiance, his eyes were full of heavenly light. The future seemed unfolded before his gaze.

Then in solemn accents, in a slow measured voice, he spoke,

"It shall be, but not yet. Through a sea of tribulation, through much darkness, they shall walk till the end arrives. The day *shall* come when Catholics in this land will go forth free, when the children of those who have wronged us shall flock to the Church's feet. O, courage, Sisters, and let us suffer; for verily it is not in vain—let us be content to sow the seed, watering it with blood and tears. Let others gather the harvest when we, by God's mercy, are garnered in the Eternal Home above. Sisters, the hour shall come—my words are like one who speaketh dreams, yet they are true—the hour shall come when on this very spot the Immaculate Conception of Mary shall have great honor, and the Sacred Heart of Love a glorious shrine. Not a tear that has been shed, not a prayer you have offered up, shall be lost or forgotten. Those who are yet unborn shall thank you, and praise the Lord through the ages of eternity."

He blessed them and passed away. He bent his steps along Piccadilly to the palace, unaware that his movements were watched and his footsteps dogged.

As he left the Grange, the nuns gazed after him and said: "Who knoweth? When his prophecy is fulfilled, and the shrine for the Heart of Jesus and His spotless Mother stands in this wild spot, perchance his image, as of one reckoned among the saints, shall gladden the eyes of the faithful even more than his look and voice, that seem to come from heaven, have gladdened our feeble hearts in this our hour of need."

CHAPTER XXV.

A PEARL OF GREAT PRICE.

THE evening shades were beginning to gather, the sun in all
its glory was about to sink in
the horizon, when a travelling
carriage, covered with mud and dust, and
drawn by tired horses, slowly rumbled
through the streets of the little town of
Paray-le-Monial, and halted before the Convent of the Saintes Maries, as the Visitation
nuns were then called. From the coach
three persons descended; and, when they
had entered the parlor and thrown off their
travelling gear, we might recognize our three
friends—Henriette de Marigny, Alethea
Howard and Marguerite.

A grille with open bars ran along one side
of the room; and, in a few minutes, the cur-
tain was withdrawn, and the Mère de
Saumaise, then Reverend Mother, welcomed
the strangers.

"Not strangers to me," said she, "but long

ago taken into my heart, since, from the letters of our good Father de la Colombière, you are well known to me. And are you, really, all come hither to join our community?"

"Such are our wishes and desires, Reverend Mother," answered Henriette; "but, speaking chiefly for myself, I feel that it will be a wonderful grace if God indeed finds me worthy of such a state."

"Well," said Mère de Saumaise, "the first thing is to give you the rest you all need after your long journey. Our extern Sisters will take care of you, and to-morrow we shall meet again."

On the following day, the three friends were admitted within the enclosure; and, after visiting the nuns' choir, the Reverend Mother led them into the garden. This garden was large, and well laid out with walks and alleys—a peaceful spot, where the soul could raise herself from the troubles of earth, and soar away in thought awhile to the heavenly garden where one day she shall rest at her will.

As the Superior and her companions pursued their path, they saw a nun in the distance pacing slowly along. As they drew near her, Mère de Saumaise spoke.

"Sister Margaret Mary," she said; and the religious instantly came to her side. With feelings of mingled curiosity and awe, the three travellers gazed on the face of her to whom, as they knew, Father de la Colombière believed our Lord had spoken. There was no natural beauty in the features, no signs of rare intellect or genius written on the brow, but the eyes were lustrous with a light from some hidden source. The friends said to themselves, as we all have said at some time or another in our lives when we have met a saint, "Those eyes have seen God." Just now, those eyes of Margaret Mary were raised to the face of her Superior, to learn her bidding, with the mild, wistful gaze of a little child.

"Sister," said the Mother, "greet these strangers; they have journeyed far. Two are of English blood, the other hath sojourned long in England, and all are the spiritual children of our honored Fa her de la Colombière."

Sister Margaret's face was lit up with a smile so bright and radiant that it made her features absolutely beautiful.

"I will leave them awhile with you, Sister," continued the Superior, "for I have press of occupation. Do you lead them to the *bosquet* hard by, where I know you love to sit, and entertain them as best you may."

Under the shade of the little bosquet, or bower, was a rough seat, on which the little group placed themselves, and began to speak of Father de la Colombière and his life in London. With tender interest the nun listened. And, when they spoke of Father de la Colombière's sermons, and how by this means the devotion to the Sacred Heart had been taught, and was beginning to take root in England, her pale face lit up with such a glow of love, of joy and of triumph, that the travellers gazed in wonder. A mother who hears that the head of her only child is crowned with the laurels he has won, the wife of one whom the world delighteth to honor, is not so full of joy and exultation as this gentle creature and passionate lover of Jesus Christ.

The generation among whom she lived
was stiff-necked and perverse.   England
was lost to the Faith—Ireland trodden down
under the oppressor's foot—France sowing
the crop of vice, worldliness, cruelty to the
poor, neglect of God, that was a century
later to bring forth a bitter harvest.   There
were many cold hearts around, even in the
sanctuary and cloister; but within this virgin
soul a divine fire had been lit which was to
inflame the whole Christian world.   Here
was one at least who did indeed know how
to love much.   On every side spread the
waters dark and drear; but, amid the waste
of sin, of coldness, of neglect, a pearl, whose
lustre the whole world was one day to
admire, shone brightly, like a star.

During the next few days, the three
friends sought each in turn private inter-
views with Sister Margaret.   She being com-
manded by her Superior to speak to each
her mind, did so.   Both Henriette de Marigny
and Alethea Howard entered the novitiate.
Marguerite took up her abode in the out-
quarters of the convent, determining to
spend a certain time in prayer and reflection
on her future course.

CHAPTER XXVI.

PHILIP TAKES HIS REVENGE.

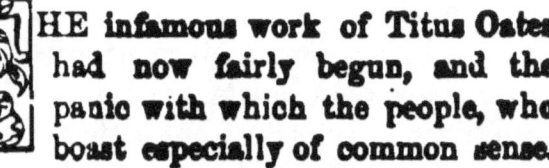

THE infamous work of Titus Oates had now fairly begun, and the panic with which the people, who boast especially of common sense, are wont to be seized by fits and starts, ran riot in the kingdom. Another gunpowder plot, only more insidious, more deadly, and more widespread, was declared by Titus Oates to be nipped in the bud and public opinion loudly demanded the punishment of those whom this villain without character or a shadow of proof accused as he would.

Father de la Colombière spent much time alone in his room. Since the commencement of the uproar he had, at the request of the Duchess of York, rarely quitted his apartments save to go to the chapel. After the arrest of his provincial and brethren, the dispersion of the nuns, and the terror and distress among Catholics, the Father had redoubled his prayers and penances. If, using our privilege as an historian, we venture to look into his sleeping chamber, which adjoined the room where he sat and received visitors, we might fancy ourselves in the cell of an anchorite. The room was perfectly bare. A few planks formed the bed. Underneath them were concealed rude instruments of penance. Often nearly the whole night was spent by him in vigils; and on one occasion, shortly after the departure of the nuns from the Grange, the Father was so rapt in prayer that the hours fleeted by unnoticed. He did not hear heavy steps ascending the stairs and pacing the corridor, till at last a violent knocking at the door aroused him. He had not time to do more than rise from his knees when the door was rudely burst open, and about a dozen soldiers, headed by an officer, rushed into the room. With perfect composure Father de la Colombière gazed at them.

"Surrender, in the King's name," cried the officer, striking the priest rudely on the shoulder. "You are summoned before the Parliament of England, you foul conspirator, you hatcher of plots against the weal of King and kingdom ! "

The man's face was scowling with rage; his teeth gnashed together as he spoke. Father de la Colombière recognized Philip Engelby, and a prayer like unto the divine " Father, forgive them, for they know not what they do," went up to heaven from the priest's heart.

" Can I take anything with me ? " demanded he, gently.

"Nothing," cried Philip, furiously. "All your papers shall be examined, and your villainy made plain. You are unmasked at last, sir; and now," he added, in a low hiss, " I have my revenge."

The Father bowed his head.

" Lead on," he said, " I am ready."

Philip gave the signal, and the party moved out. Thirteen or more soldiers were there to guard one fragile-looking, delicate priest. Philip kept close to his side, muttering, as he strode along, oaths, curses, and abuse of all kinds. Like his Master, the confessor for His name was silent, but with every blasphemy which wounded the Heart

of Jesus as it fell from the lips of a creature
He had died to redeem, rose up an act of
reparation from a being whom that same
redemption had made a saint.

Along the silent deserted streets they went,
often stumbling on their way into holes and
ruts, for the light thrown from the torch
carried by a soldier cast an uncertain gleam.
Father de la Colombière was greatly exhausted when the party reached Newgate.
He was thrust into a cell, the door locked upon
him, and he was left alone in the darkness
in a small, damp, and perfectly unfurnished
room. He sunk on his knees, but weariness
overcame him, and he was compelled to lie
down. The damp of the place struck his
always delicate lungs like a knife. A violent
fit of coughing ensued, and when he removed
the handkerchief from his mouth, it was
stained with blood.

When the day came, he was visited by the
jailor. Bread and water were served out to
him; and, in the course of the day, a wooden
stool and a sack of straw were given for his
use. He was allowed no light save the
glimmer of day that flickered in through a

narrow slit in the wall; no writing materials, no means of communication with his friends. Fortunately, he had in his pocket his Breviary; and thus, in vocal and mental prayer, the first days of his captivity passed away.

On the third day, he was brought before the Committee of the House of Lords; and, as the prisoner was brought in, many faces confronted him. Some were dark with fury, others were full of scorn. There was not one pitying glance as the slight form of the priest, all covered with the dust and dirt of his prison, stood before them.

What a victim he seemed in the gaze of these stately men—feeble in body, of another race than theirs, poor and friendless, for none dared to raise a voice in his favor. Why does he not tremble before them? Does he not know his fate is in their hands? He stands without support—not defiant, but as one who has nothing to fear —not downcast, but as one whose soul is anchored in peace. There is no contempt or triumph in his look, and yet men feel he is their master. There is a calm majesty they cannot subdue. They can kill the body—no hard task to complete the work that penance and mortification have begun. They can soon destroy that fragile frame, which is but like "a lamp to hold a soul." But they cannot conquer the spirit. Among them, even now, he is a king.

Father de la Colombière being placed at the bar, an indictment was read declaring he was involved in a conspiracy to dethrone King Charles, place the Duke of York on the throne, and establish the Popish religion in the country.

"Guilty or not guilty?" said the Clerk of Arraigns.

"Not guilty," answered the prisoner.

The Jesuit listened in silence while he was accused of words and deeds foreign to his nature, his religion and his rule. A light had been seen burning at midnight in his chamber, the window of which looked on the Place of St. James. It denoted meetings of conspirators. His steps had been tracked to and from a lonely farm-house near May Fair. The house had been searched, and was found empty; but some morsels of torn, half-burnt paper picked up

gave evidence it had been the haunt of
traitors. It was believed that several hundred persons had been reconciled to the
Popish religion by this man. It was further
deposed that a young Frenchman, a native
of Dauphiné, would give important evidence
against the prisoner; and, accordingly,
Arsène came forward.

But it now transpired that his name was
not Arsène, but Olivier du Fiquet, and his
statement was as follows:

"La Colombière, Jesuit and preacher to
the Duchess, hath, for the space of three
months, had frequent communication with
Mr. Coleman, who came every day to com-
municate with him in his chamber from
eleven in the morning till midday.

"Further, that Monsieur la Colombière
sent his servant Lièvre to stay in the country for the space of two months and a half,
and took to his service the nephew of Mr.
Coleman, betwixt thirteen and fourteen years
old.

"And after that Mr. Coleman was put in
prison, Monsieur la Colombière took his servant again and sent away the nephew of Mr.
Coleman, and went to live in the country.

"Further, I know that Monsieur la Colombière hath great correspondence with Father la Chaise and with Cardinal Bouillon.

"2. Monsieur la Colombière told me—to induce me to his religion—that if I made so much difficulty the King would not hinder me to make choice of the Roman Catholic religion, seeing he knew very well that the King was a Catholic in his heart.

"3. Furthermore, when I represented to him 'that the Parliament would not suffer perversion in England,' Monsieur la Colombière said to me that if the Parliament opposed Roman Catholics the King would dissolve it. And further, that the Parliament should not be always master. He told me also 'that I should see in a little time all England changed,' which also was confirmed to me by his servant.

"4. And, as I had a design to go study at Oxford, he turned me from it in representing to me that if I went to study at Oxford I should fill my mind with the errors which the divinity at Oxford teacheth, contrary to Holy Scripture; and if I would return to France he would, by means of Father la

Chaise, Jesuit, and confessor to the King of
France, place me to study in the College of
Clermont; and also that he did write to
Paris to a Jesuit in the absence of Father la
Chaise, whose answer I read myself in Mon-
sieur la Colombière's chamber; and also that
I had told the Duke of York that he had
turned me from my purpose of being a
minister, and said that his Highness ex-
pressed much satisfaction in it, which sur-
prised me much. But then Monsieur la
Colombière told me 'that I ought not to
wonder at that, seeing his Highness was a
Catholic, and received often the Sacrament.'
This also was confirmed to me by his servant.

"5. Moreover, Monsieur la Colombière hath
received many abjurations in his chamber, as
well of French as of English; and also I
spoke in his chamber to an English gentleman, whom he sent into France to pervert
by means of Cardinal Bouillon.

"6. That Monsieur Drevil, a Frenchman,
carried to Monsieur la Colombière an English merchant, to pervert him, whom La
Colombière was to send into France, and his
family to the Cardinal Bouillon.

"7. That Monsieur la Colombière sends secretly priests into Virginia, amongst others Maccarty, an Irish priest, who was carried by La Colombière's servant, and by his orders, to Monsieur la Choquenna, who lives at the Savoy; and also La Colombière told me that he desired to go thither. This is all that I can confirm upon oath.

"8. Furthermore, that La Colombière hath made Mass to be said at Mr. Angus' by Maccarty every Sunday and holiday, and also in the country.

"9. That La Colombière hath seduced Monsieur Salamon, a minister at the Savoy, to put him into a convent; and another person that was come with an intention to enter into the ministry, La Colombière hath sent them into France, and gave them money in Picardy in his servant Lièvre's house, and then they were to pass to Rome by the means of Cardinal Bouillon.

"This is all I can affirm upon oath, and in the presence of the parties." *

---

* The above is historical. It is extracted from "Records of the English Province, S.J.," by Brother Foley, S.J.

These words caused a great sensation in the House; and the prisoner, for the first time making any movement, turned his eyes on Olivier. The young man flushed painfully and turned away his head.

The Lord Chancellor, however, now spoke.

"We have heard enough. Prisoner at the bar, have you anything to say in your defence?"

"The charges, my lord, laid against me are mainly false."

"O, *mainly!*" cried one knot of peers; "not wholly or entirely."

"What matter what the knave saith," exclaimed another; "know we not these villains are trained to lie?"

"Pass sentence on him, my lord," cried a third; "hanging is too good for folks like these."

"Hold!" exclaimed an old man, who had not hitherto spoken; "have a care what you are about. This man is a Frenchman, and what will King Louis say?"

The remark struck home. A whispered consultation went on for a few minutes, and the Father was ordered back to prison.

CHAPTER XXVII.

MARY BEATRICE'S DREAM.

WHILE Father de la Colombière lingered in prison, Lady Edenhall was at the height of her power. The mutual hatred which both she and Philip Engelby had conceived for the Jesuit had brought them together, and Lady Edenhall's darling wish was fulfilled of seeing Philip once more her slave. Lord Edenhall had long since found out that his wife cared not a straw for him, but only for his name and fortune. Leaving her, therefore, to the enjoyment of these, he wrapped himself up more than ever in State affairs, grew morose and silent, and the Earl and Countess rarely met.

Lady Edenhall had it all her own way. She had never looked more beautiful and magnificent than at an evening reception of the Duchess of York. Mary Beatrice had no mind for festivities when her chaplain was in prison, and her best friends scattered

and persecuted; but she dared not show
signs of grief, and the Duke insisted on
giving more receptions than usual, in order
to feign indifference to the state of public
affairs.

The card-tables were arranged as usual,
but the Duchess had refused to play, making
some smiling excuse which would have
passed current, more especially as of late
her card-playing had notably diminished.

In her heart Mary Beatrice said:

"No, not while *he* is languishing in prison
will I disobey his counsel. Gladly would I
forget in the excitement of cards the aching
pain at my heart, but I will not do it."

Presently Lady Edenhall approached her.

"Your Highness does not play to-night,"
she said, in dulcet tones.

"No," answered Mary Beatrice, quickly
toying with her bracelet; "I am not in the
humor to-night."

"Have orders, then, come even from Newgate?" demanded the Countess. "Then
may we say indeed of your Highness' holy
chaplain, though silent yet he speaketh."

Mary Beatrice started and colored deeply.

No soul save herself had known of Father de la Colombière's counsel. She trembled, and looked up into Lady Edenhall's face.

"Has he been *tortured?*" she faltered, while her cheeks, erewhile flushed crimson, turned deadly pale.

"Not yet, Princess, but he may; and he shall, if he interferes with your Highness' pleasure."

Mary Beatrice rose and walked to a card-table. A game was just concluded, and she soon made up her set. In a few moments she was absorbed in play. Never had she been so excited. Her eyes shone, her cheeks flushed, her bosom heaved. No one would recognize the graceful Princess, the weeping novice torn from her convent to be an unwilling bride, the pious listener to Father de la Colombière's sermons. This was a gambler. It was easy to foresee what Mary Beatrice could and would become if this passion were indulged.

Lady Edenhall bent over her for a few minutes with a gratified look—such as a fiend might have worn in the flesh—and then she turned away.

"I will labor at this," she murmured to herself. "I will undo his work in that soul. I will ruin his fair hopes of her. She is easily depressed. I believe I could get her in time to abjure her creed, and then—and then—I think I should wipe out the disgrace of having once knelt at his feet. Faugh! I hate myself as I think of it. How heated these rooms are! I feel faint, actually."

And going towards an entrance, she sought the corridor. Philip Engelby, always on the watch, hastened after her.

"I feel unwell, Phil," said she; "bring me a chair. Sitting here in the air will refresh me."

Philip brought a seat, and Lady Edenhall emptied her bottle of essences.

"Dost thou know, Phil," she continued, "I have dismissed Olivier du Fiquet to day? The fellow was too insolent, too presuming. We have already paid him beyond his deserts; but it seems he thought we were to endow him with a fortune and make him equal with ourselves. Imagine!"—and Lady Edenhall laughed scornfully—"he hinted I was to let

him come to these receptions, and try his
luck at winning a wife. He thinks his
handsome face should carry all before it.
So I bade him go help the cooks and scul-
lions, and choose his wife from them. Victoire, the head cook, is his countrywoman,
and a vastly pretty damsel."

"What did he say to that?" inquired
Philip. "You have courage, Di. I would
not have dared to stir up his fiery blood."

"He went away in a fury," she answered,
"saying, perhaps this would be my last visit
to St. James'. I do believe he will tell some
tale to my lord. Poor fool! he little
knoweth Edenhall." And the Countess
laughed merrily. "In truth, though," she
said presently, "I do not feel well. I have
taken a chill. Escort me, Phil, and call my
people. I will hie me to bed."

The reception at St. James' was over, and
the palace was silent, its inmates probably
wrapped in sleep.

Mary Beatrice had gone to bed with fevered
blood and aching heart. For the first time
in her life she had tried to drown the voice

of conscience. Hitherto her religion had
been that of the loving child who, having
erred, runs to his father's feet to tell his fault
and receive his pardon. God had been to
her a tender Father, listening to the faintest
word of contrition that fell from her lips.
To-night, for the first time, she shunned His
face. She knelt not before her crucifix; she
did not kiss the feet of her Madonna; she
sprinkled no holy water on her bed.
Hurriedly undressing, she buried her face
in the pillows. On a table near lay the
heap of glittering gold she had won at play.
She fell into a fevered sleep, and her guardian
angel raised his eyes to the Face which he
always beheld, and cried:

"Shall this fair blossom wither beneath
the world's scorching glare? O, by her
long fidelity, by her deeds of charity, and by
her acts of humility, have pity on Thy
child!"

Some hours afterwards, the waiting-
women, who slept in the ante-room to the
Duchess' chamber, were awakened by loud
cries. They rushed to their mistress. She
was crouching on the ground trembling in

terror, her long raven hair flowing around her, her hands clasped in convulsive agony. She could not speak; and, when the women raised her up, covered her with blankets, and tried to soothe her, her terrified eyes wandered round the room as if she saw some frightful vision. It was some time before she could speak.

"I have had," said she, at length, "a frightful dream.* I dare not tell you unless you swear not to betray me."

The women eagerly swore, and the Duchess, with trembling accents, went on to say:

"By my bedside stood Lady Diana, but changed—O, awfully changed! She was enveloped in flames, and her eyes glared like those of a wild beast. She said—O!" cried Mary Beatrice, "shall I ever forget that voice?"—*'I am damned! I am in the flames of hell!'* "

"And did your Highness speak to her?" asked the trembling maids.

---

* This dream of Mary Beatrice is an historical incident in her life. The time of its occurrence, and the person of whom she dreamt, have been altered for the purpose of our tale.

"Yea, and with a strange courage, at which I now marvel, I said, 'How can this be? I cannot believe it.'"

"And then?" demanded the servants.

But another fit of shuddering seized on the Duchess, and she was so nearly fainting that the women had to give her a cordial ere her white lips could frame a sentence. When she spoke again, she said:

"The spectre answered, 'Madame, to convince you, feel my hand;' and she laid her hand upon my arm. It burnt and scorched me with such exceeding anguish that I cried out and awoke."

"But, dearest madam," said Alix la Motte, "It is impossible. Lady Edenhall is in life and health. She was at the reception."

"I know, I know," answered Mary Beatrice; and then into her memory there flashed Lady Edenhall's last words and last glance. She had done a devil's work for Mary Beatrice's soul. With a resolution which belonged to her character, although it was at the same time gentle and yielding, Mary Beatrice disengaged herself from the sheltering arms of Alix and Blanche, and walked with bare feet to the crucifix, which hung above her prie-dieu. She fell down before it in mute and voiceless prayer. Her pious attendants knelt beside her.

What passed in the soul of the Princess was known only to God, but doubtle-s a deep contrition was breathed from that gentle heart, and a mighty resolution taken. From that day Mary Beatrice never again touched cards.

At last Alix, getting alarmed, persuaded her mistress to go to bed. The fright and the sudden chill made her ill; and, when morning came, she was unfit to rise. Lying faint and weary on her pillows, she did not see the scared faces of her women, nor hear Alix's determined resistance in the anteroom in refusing admission to visitors brimful with news. But Alix's power availed nothing when the Duke of York, hearing his wife was ill, came to see her. He went quickly into the chamber, and, taking her little hand in his, said kindly:

"Has this awful news upset you, sweetheart? Poor Laly Diana! I can hardly credit it. She, so full of life yestereven, lieth now a blackened corpse. What! did you not hear it?" as his wife's eyes, distended with terror, were fixed on his face. "She is dead; and by foul play, they whisper. The body is turning black already—the effect of some strong poison. She was found dead in her bed, and must have been so for some hours. Ha, Alix, Blanche! hasten hither! I have been too rough! Her Highness has fainted."

CHAPTER XXVIII.

REAPING THE HARVEST.

OR several days Mary Beatrice's illness continued, and the story of her dream was bruited about, causing great indignation in the minds of many Protestants, but having a salutary effect on some Catholics ready to forsake the faith for this world's goods. That Lady Edenhall had been poisoned there was no manner of doubt. It was supposed some slight portion had been mixed with a delicate dish of which she had partaken before going to the palace, and a larger dose with the succory-water that always stood by her bedside to be taken in the night. Feeling feverish, she had emptied the glass, and an agonizing death had quickly followed. In the blackened corpse with protruding eyes, an object of shuddering dread to the domestics that but the day before had trembled at her frown, who could recognize the haughty beauty, Diana Edenhall? With

a loud voice the mute corpse cried, "Have pity upon me, my friends, have pity upon me; for the hand of the Lord hath touched me." But among those she called her friends there was none to pity her. It was only from the lips of him she deemed her enemy (hearing the news in his prison cell) that there went up a cry of anguish for her soul.

Olivier du Fiquet had disappeared; so also had many of Lady Edenhall's jewels. Search was made for him in vain; and a whisper that Philip Engelby, for reasons of his own, had favored his flight, reached Lord Edenhall's ears, and Philip was called to account. High words passed between them, for which Philip demanded satisfaction. A duel was fought, with rancor on each side. The combatants were skilled swordsmen, and both were borne from the field sorely wounded, and in a few hours Philip Engelby died, with a curse on his lips. Lord Edenhall was maimed for life, and rendered a hopeless invalid.

About a week after Philip's death Father de la Colombière was again summoned b.....

the House of Lords. His time of imprisonment had greatly changed him. A sharp
cough shook his frame, and he looked little
more than skin and bone; but his glorious
eyes shone brightly in his pale worn face,
and there was no sign of fear, of faltering, of
dismay to be seen on his features. Detained
for some hours in an ante-chamber, until
"my lords" should summon him to their
presence, he quietly took out his Breviary
and recited the office for the day.

He was not, however, brought again before
the tribunal. "My lords" probably felt
somewhat ashamed of having to confess that
the accusations laid against him could not
be substantiated. Great things had been
hoped for by the imprisonment of her Highness' chaplain. His papers had been narrowly examined, but, like his Master, no
witness, save false witness, could be found
against him.

At last an officer of the King's guard
entered the ante-chamber, and displayed his
warrant from the King to banish Claude de
la Colombière, "a pestilent Jesuit," from the
kingdom, and to witness his embarkation.

The Father bowed his head, and, closing his Breviary, was about to put it in his pocket, when the officer roughly seized his arm and hustled him before him.   The book fell on the ground.*

It was a bitter day, with showers of sleet and a keen east wind. Ere the Jesuit and his guards had proceeded far the former tottered in his walk, and then fell to the ground.   He was raised up, and a stream of blood was flowing from his mouth.

The officer felt alarmed. The death of this prisoner, even by sickness, would be a disaster involving King Charles in a disagreeable manner with King Louis. The insensible form was carried into an hostelry, and word was taken to the palace; upon which the King (only too glad personally to grant the favor) accorded ten days of repose and liberty before Father de la Colombière should be obliged to quit the kingdom. Moreover, he was permitted to lodge with

---

* There is a tradition that a Missal and Breviary belonging to Father de la Colombière were left in England, and were at one time in possession of Sion College. No trace of them now exists.

Father Russell, the Franciscan, one of her Majesty's chaplains, and as yet protected by the marriage contract of Queen Catharine from the prevailing storm.

With devoted kindness, Father Russell did all in his power to restore the shattered frame of his friend; and in a day or two Father de la Colombière was able, to his great joy, as he tells us in his letters, to bid adieu to many who had known and loved him. Thus he gained access to those of his brethren then languishing in Newgate.

The Provincial, Father Whitbread, had been taken from a sick-bed, where he was suffering from low fever, cast into a dark, damp cell, and loaded with chains. But, when Father de la Colombière entered his cell, the face he gazed on was radiant with happiness.

"And so, Father Provincial," said Father de la Colombière, "you were right, and I was wrong. You foresaw a storm was at hand; I thought peace and increase were to be given unto your province."

"Yes," said Father Whitbread; "I know not why, but an interior conviction has been in my mind for years that troubles were at hand. When I witnessed the success God was pleased to give to your preaching and ministry among souls, I tried to combat the feeling as a mistrust of God's providence. But ever since the Friday after Corpus Christi, when we made the consecration of ourselves to the Sacred Heart of Jesus, the conviction hath grown stronger."

"And that is why you preached so earnestly to *Ours* at Liège on the Feast of St. James-- was it not?"

"I could not help it, Father," replied the Provincial. "When I looked on the group of young fervent souls renewing their vows unto the Lord, my heart was moved within me, and the words of that day's Gospel seemed so appropriate to the occasion: '*Can you drink the chalice that I shall drink? They say unto Him, We can.*' And so I went on to ask them: 'Can you undergo a hard persecution? Are you contented to be falsely betrayed, and injured, and hurried away to prison?' 'We can: blessed be God!' 'Can you suffer the hardships of a jail? Can you sleep on straw, and live on hard diet? Can you lie in chains and fetters? Can you endure the rack?' 'We can: blessed be God!' 'Can you be brought to the bar, and hear yourselves falsely sworn against? Can you patiently receive the sentence of an unjust judge condemning you to a painful and ignominious death—to be hanged, drawn and quartered?' 'We can: blessed be God!' These words flowed from my lips without my will, as it were; but they affrighted none of those ardent souls, and I comfort myself in thinking that, when we are cut down, others shall take our places."

"I have brought you comfort, Father," said his visitor. "I shall leave with you seven Hosts, that you may, for a week to come, feast upon the Bread of the strong."

A heavenly smile lit up the Provincial's face as he took the Sacred Gift from the hands of his brother in Christ.

"Wonderful is the grace of our God," he continued. "Often do I mind me of the words of our Master, '*Your joy no man can take from you.*' What is this dark cell, these chains, this feebleness of body, when

Christ consoleth me? Thanks be to Him,
I shall die by His grace in the bosom of the
Society, my true mother. From my infancy
in her arms, I was taught that practice of
mental prayer which, having become habitual
to me, is now my comfort and support."

"Yes," said Father de la Colombière, "we
may say of meditation, as did Holy David,
'Sweeter than honey unto my mouth.' Tell
me, my Reverend Father, I beg of you—for
we are about to part for ever—does God
bestow on you many lights in prayer?"

"He is very good to me," answered the
old man. "My spirit travels with Him
amidst the hills and seas of Galilee. I seem
to live with Him on earth, to hear His voice,
to touch His hands. What are sufferings?
What is death? The affair of a moment,
and then I enjoy Him for all eternity of
whom only to think of on earth is bliss. . . .
Is your time drawing near to leave me,
Father? Confess me, an it pleases, you,
before you go."

Father de la Colombière visited the following day Father Barrow, more generally called
Harcourt, the Rector of the London College

of the Society. The old gray-haired Father of seventy years was bright and happy as a child. To die a martyr's death had been, as he told Father de la Colombière, his daily prayer for twenty years; and now God was about to grant the desire of his heart, and he praised and blessed His holy name.

Then Father de la Colombière visited Father John Caldwell and Father Anthony Turner, both converts (the latter a B.A. of Cambridge), and Father John Gawan, who in his novitiate had been called "the Angel," on account of his childlike innocence and candor.

Having heard the confessions of these his dear brethren, and bestowed on each a gift similar to that he had given the Provincial, Father de la Colombière visited also Father Mico, "socius" to the Provincial, and Father Mumford, both of whom shortly afterwards died while in the act of prayer, worn out by the weight of their irons. The five other Fathers whom we have mentioned, after a long imprisonment, were executed at Tyburn, and gained the crown of martyrdom. So also did many other Fathers of the Society and of other religious orders, and secular priests, apprehended and executed in London and other towns. The aged Jesuit, Father Neville, whose years numbered eighty-four, was flung down stairs by the pursuivants, and so went to heaven.

Father de la Colombière managed to gain admission to the Tower, where Lord Stafford was confined, and bestowed all the comfort he could on the brave old nobleman. He saw Katherine Howard, who, with her mother, had taken up her abode in a narrow lodging close to the Tower, that they might enjoy daily access to their beloved one, and relieve, as far as might be, his wants.

The Father did not fail to visit the Duchess of York, and this at the earnest request of the Duke, who feared his wife's mind would never recover from the effect of her frightful dream. But to her troubled spirit her chaplain brought help and consolation. He foresaw that Mary Beatrice had a thorny path to tread, and must not lose her courage for what might be only an imagination.

"Pray for this poor soul," said he, "and let

as not presume to judge that which is hidden in the secrets of God."

Then at last the holy Claude de la Colombière bade farewell to the land in which he had labored, prayed and suffered. He bent his steps to Paray-le-Monial, where he spent a few days, and then hastened to report himself to his Provincial at Lyons. Having told Marguerite of her father's state, he approved of her resolve to return to England and devote herself to that father's solace.

Lord Edenhall lingered for two years, a fretful and suffering being. He was removed to Edenhall; and often did good Mistress Dorothy marvel to see the once gay and impetuous Marguerite changed into the patient, unselfish nurse and dutiful child.

In the dark waters of affliction, this pearl at length shone brightly. She had her reward when death drew near. A salutary fear of God's judgments came on the proud old man. He cried out for mercy; and, by Marguerite's contrivance, a priest stood beside him, and reconciled the parting soul.

About the same time, Lord Stafford, at the end of two years' imprisonment, was beheaded

on Tower Hill, on the Feast of St. Thomas
of Canterbury, 1680. His wife did not long
survive him; and Katherine and Marguerite,
linking their fates together, went to Paris.
There, some years after, Lady Katherine
married, and became the excellent wife and
mother that all who knew her could have
anticipated.

Marguerite entered the Convent of the
Conception, and was sent, after her profes-
sion, to a hospital served by the Sisters of
her institute. Her duties led her to attend
a man suffering frightful agonies from cancer
in the mouth. He obstinately refused to
speak to a priest, and lay mostly in a sort of
gloomy stupor, save when, in paroxysms of
anger, he wildly blasphemed. One day, an
Englishman, happening to visit the hospital, was conducted by Sister Mary Austin
(our Marguerite) through the ward. As
they drew near the sufferer's bed, they were
speaking in English. The wild start the
man gave, the agonized look he cast ere
again cowering down in his bed, convinced
the Sister a chord might be touched. When
the visitor was gone, she sat by this poor

creature, and spoke in English. By degrees, in subsequent visits, she contrived to break the ice. It was Olivier du Fiquet, the traitor, the murderer. With great diffi- culty, she persuaded him to listen to a priest; and, as soon after he became, from his dread malady, speechless, absolution was given conditionally, and he was anointed. He could not receive Holy Communion, and his death-agony was one of those fright- ful scenes upon which the mind cannot dwell.

Father de la Colombière survived his return to France little more than three years, during which time he was a constant invalid. His health never recovered the effect of his imprisonment, and he may be truly reckoned among the martyrs to the Faith in England. He died at Paray-le- Monial, February 15, 1682.

Both Henriette de Marigny and Alethea Howard were among the most fervent of the holy community of which God bestowed the singular gift of becoming the cradle of devotion to the Sacred Heart of Jesus.

Our task is well-nigh done. Yet, let us
linger in the spots where once lived and
suffered those we have written of. May
Fair is now a fashionable quarter of the
town; but, hard by, on the spot where once
stood the Grange, or *Farm*, is a shrine dear
to many hearts, and which has to many
proved the threshold of eternal life. Raised
in honor of Mary's Immaculate Conception,
her dear name is held in constant reverence
and renown, and the fairest flowers blossom
at her feet. And within that shrine there is
a spot embalmed with love and prayer. Here,
on the pictured wall, are the forms of Claude
de la Colombière and his spiritual child,
Blessed Margaret Mary. There burn the
lamps before the Sacred Heart. How many
tears have been dried, how many hearts consoled, how many battles against our spiritual
foes fought and won, in that spot, none but
God and His angels can tell.

There are those who believe an earnest
prayer in that sanctuary is never left unheard; and no wonder. In the midst of the
vast, wicked Babylon, the angels of the Lord
keep watch, and remind Him who rewards

so grandly of the love, the patience, the prayers, the sufferings, of those who have gone before. They labored, and we have entered into the fruit of their labors. May we be faithful to our trust! And, if the hour of peace be over, may we be ready in our turn to suffer and to die, if need be, for the honor of the Heart of Jesus, and of the Mother whom that Heart loves so well!

THE END.

www.ingramcontent.com/pod-product-compliance
Lightning Source LLC
Chambersburg PA
CBHW031421020726
47499CB00005B/1534